DARK INHERITANCE

DARK INHERITANCE

Elaine Feinstein

Chivers Press   •   Thorndike Press
Bath, England   Waterville, Maine USA

This Large Print edition is published by Chivers Press, England, and by Thorndike Press, USA.

Published in 2001 in the U.K. by arrangement with The Women's Press, Ltd.

Published in 2001 in the U.S. by arrangement with The Women's Press.

U.K. Hardcover   ISBN 0–7540–4623–0 (Chivers Large Print)
U.K. Softcover   ISBN 0–7540–4624–9 (Camden Large Print)
U.S. Softcover   ISBN 0–7862–3566–7 (General Series Edition)

The text of this Large Print edition is unabridged.
Other aspects of the book may vary from the original edition.

Set in 16 pt. New Times Roman.

Printed in Great Britain on acid-free paper.

British Library Cataloguing in Publication Data available

Library of Congress Cataloging-in-Publication Data

Feinstein, Elaine.
    Dark inheritance / Elaine Feinstein.
       p.   cm.
    ISBN 0–7862–3566–7 (lg. print : sc : alk. paper)
    1. Mothers and sons—Fiction. 2. Rome (Italy)—Fiction.
    3. Interviewing—Fiction. 4. Novelists—Fiction. 5. Large type
    books. I. Title.
    PR6056.E38 D37 2001
    823'.914—dc21   2001041494

CHAPTER ONE

It was raining heavily over the City of London as Rachel O'Malley found a space to park her Vauxhall Corsa, just south of the river. There were few people on the streets, though the shops at the tube station were not yet closed. Over a railway bridge, trains went by without stopping. It was a townscape more reminiscent of New York than London. A few boys in T-shirts were standing in the doorway of a TV rental shop, watching a football game. Seeing her consult the map in her hand, they called out coarse suggestions of how to help.

*   *   *

Rachel was elegantly thin; in another age she might have been thought too thin; you could see the delicacy of her bones at shoulder and wrist. And yet her tiny breasts were plump, their nipples easy to guess under her silk blouse. She wore subtle colours: browns and blues together, dark greens. Her black hair curled softly round her face, her blue eyes looked the bluer for the lapis necklace at her throat. At forty, however, she was at least fifteen years older than the boys imagined.

*   *   *

She had been one of the stars of her generation at Cambridge; poets, rugby players, and sons of dukes fell in love with her. And not only for her beauty. Rachel was the child of glamorous parents: her mother a lovely, feckless child of the aristocracy, her father the writer Frank O'Malley, whose urbane, elliptical novels were spiced with all the scurrilous charm of Fitzrovia. A brilliant future was predicted for Rachel herself. Instead, she decided to marry Christopher Cook, a formidable young professor of semiotics. It took her some time to discover how remote from her were the passions that went into his research.

*   *   *

Her own passions were diverse and contradictory. She had been a talented actress at Cambridge, and in the first year of her life in London found work in an experimental theatre company in Battersea. Then Christopher took up a university post in Norwich. She commuted for a time, still in thrall to her dream of Theatre, until Christopher was offered a chair in Scotland and she began to remember other unsatisfied ambitions. In any case, no one could commute daily between south London and Scotland, and by then there was her son Tom to think about.

Thirty miles outside Aberdeen, Rachel began to work on a scholarly book about Roman drama, while reviewing for the TLS. When she and Christopher finally separated, Tom was fourteen and Rachel paid the mortgage on a tall house in Camden Town largely by renting out rooms.

*   *   *

And what brought Rachel to this desolate piece of London that evening? The invitation of Zoe Sparks, a friend, who suggested Rachel might enjoy a glimpse of the London poetry scene. It was not a world in which Rachel felt much at home. That night in June, however, something led her to accept. It wasn't loneliness. Rachel enjoyed the freedom of living alone, and had recently brought to an end an affair with a married man. For the moment she was not looking for a new lover. She felt a bleakness closer to boredom, as if she could no longer imagine any change in the shape of her life. She told herself she was curious about the Old Operating Theatre.

*   *   *

There were a few people she knew making their way to the same event, eager to meet one another, and for the most part younger than she was; among them Zoe, who had been so

3

pressing in her invitation on the telephone but now seemed only perfunctory in her welcome. Rachel guessed she was nervously anticipating her own performance.

*   *   *

To reach the amphitheatre, visitors had to climb round a winding stair like a minaret; higher still, in the very attic, herbs hung in profusion from wooden rafters, each labelled with its properties: borage, a stiff white plant with prickly hairs, for instance, said to have the fragrance of cucumbers and thought to keep off scurvy. There was bladderwrack and bogbean, goat's-beard and meadowsweet. A poem in themselves, she thought, less pleased to examine the instruments of surgery on show in glass cases.

*   *   *

The old hospital had been there since the days before Lister, and the reading was to take place in the old operating theatre itself, the audience sitting on steeply raised racks of wooden seats to watch the poets perform beside a wooden block like a butcher's. The seats were packed because the readers were well-known and the occasion charitable, but Rachel found her attention wandering to imagine the patients who had once been

4

compelled to lie without anaesthesia on that block, awaiting the saws and pincers of surgery, and so inexorably found herself thinking of her father, who had put his trust in twentieth-century medicine and, for all the wisdom of modern science, died nevertheless, still poignantly in love with being alive, a few days short of his fifty-fourth birthday.

*   *   *

He went into hospital so the doctors could put a probe down his throat to investigate what he called his dyspepsia. Even the thought of that probe made her gag, but he had been unworried, even curious. They found a tumour the size of a small brick. From that moment on, the prognosis was never good. After his chemotherapy, he was exhausted but altogether himself; his stubbly jowls a little thinner, his expression still amused. He remained 'Frank O'Malley. Famously dying,' as he described the situation to his many visitors with a smiling irony.

*   *   *

Rachel watched people throng to her father's bedside: luminaries of newspaper and television, painters, restaurant owners, women Rachel did not know. Her father had been much loved. It was the last year of her

5

marriage to Christopher, who travelled to conferences all over the world. She had no desire to accompany him by then and cared less about his unfaithfulness than the petty quarrels that rose between them whenever he returned. When Rachel's mother flew in from Caracas after more than twenty years' absence, her frail beauty and Chanel-scented presence were a harbinger of the end. Nevertheless, Rachel told herself, staring down at the butcher's block beneath, there had been palliatives for her father. Two hundred years ago, people had endured pain and terror without relief.

*   *   *

In the amphitheatre, the first poet read and sat down again. Rachel's attention was brought back to the present by a tap on the shoulder, and she turned to recognise Ridley Martin, the new young literary editor of the Sunday Enquirer.

'Keats would have watched from these very seats,' he said. 'It's Rachel O'Malley, isn't it? Didn't you have a book out about Roman theatre last year?'

*   *   *

Ridley Martin looked about twenty-three. His fair complexion and delicate lips had made him a delicious temptation to many older boys at his public school. His sexuality remained ambivalent. Rachel had known his elder brother slightly at Cambridge, but Ridley was altogether sharper and more ambitious. She was surprised he knew about her book, which had made little stir even in the academic press.

*   *   *

So then, in the interval, they stood talking about Ovid and Horace, and why there was no Sappho among the Roman poets: and what the hell Seneca the moralist was doing when he wrote his plays about murderous passions, until Rachel mentioned the recent Emanuel Cellini novel and the unease she had felt reading it, as if some personal taboo were being broken.

*   *   *

'An odd book to turn into a bestseller,' said Ridley.

'Well, it's the Phaedra story. The incest, surely?'

'No. It's because Cellini's father is an important politician. People guess the boy is writing out of his own life.'

*   *   *

7

At this Ridley's eyes had grown suddenly thoughtful.

'Now I wonder if *you* could get to him,' he murmured. 'Nobody else can. Did you notice one of the sections has an epigraph from a novel of your father's?'

She had, of course.

'I'll have to talk to someone on the magazine section.'

* * *

At this moment, a pretty young girl dressed in a zebra jacket and black pelmet skirt rushed over to embrace Ridley and pour out a flood of gossip.

'Clarissa Ferguson,' said Ridley, when there was a moment to say anything. 'And this is Rachel O'Malley. A classical scholar.'

Clarissa turned her green eyes on Rachel briefly, as if assessing her likely significance, and then turned back to Ridley without a blink.

* * *

Since Ridley seemed unlikely to return to his intriguing suggestion, Rachel moved away to join Zoe, who had been watching the encounter from the other side of the room.

'That bitch Clarissa,' she muttered. 'One year down from Oxford and look at her. It's unbearable.'

Rachel murmured something sympathetic. She had already decided not to stay for the second half of the reading. Even as she began to apologise for her departure, however, Zoe herself gave a shriek of excited solidarity and left to join another group of friends. It was then, and much to her surprise, that Rachel found Ridley Martin back at her elbow.

'Sorry we were interrupted. I haven't forgotten what we were saying. Would you like a crack at Cellini if I can fix a week in Rome?'

Before she could reply he looked at his watch. 'Damn. I'm late for a horribly solemn meeting at the Garrick. Give me your numbers and you'll hear in a day or so, if I can swing it.'

'How would I get to Emanuel Cellini if he won't see anyone?' she asked.

We'll think of someone in Rome who can help,' he promised.

*   *   *

On the way back to the car, her step was lighter and her thoughts filled with Roman sunshine. It was no longer raining in London either, though neon lights from a dry cleaner's reflected in the shine of the deserted pavement. As she turned into the street where she had parked, she had a glimpse of two burly figures, one with his arm through the triangular window at the back of her car.

9

*   *   *

'Stop it,' she called out furiously, against all common sense since she was alone in the side turning. She was, after all, slightly built and without so much as a heavy ring for a weapon, but she continued to walk purposively towards the car and the gamble paid off; the two youngsters ran off at her approach. She felt quite pleased with herself, though there was glass over the back seat and she would now have to take the car into a garage. Far from being put out by the incident, however, a completely inexplicable pool of happiness flooded her as she found herself driving over Waterloo Bridge, with the river shining quietly on either side of her and the June sky clearing over St Paul's. She had a shivery hunch. *Something* was going to happen.

*   *   *

The phone remained spectacularly silent the following day and when it did ring it was not Ridley Martin but Rachel's mother.

'I'm in London,' she said. 'With a friend.'

'Last time you passed through London, you promised to give me a few days' warning,' said Rachel ungraciously. 'You know I haven't room for two.'

'But, darling, we're staying at the

Connaught. We shan't be a *bother*. I was going to invite you for breakfast tomorrow morning, unless you're too busy.'

'I never have anything more than coffee in the morning,' said Rachel.

*   *   *

She was ashamed that her mother's drawling voice still made her blood prickle with anger. It was not as though her parents' separation had been particularly painful. Rachel's mother had never been a very substantial presence in her childhood. A visitor from a gossamer fairy world, out most nights, and a late sleeper, her departure had been more of a quiet floating away than a drama.

*   *   *

Rachel's resentment was the more inexplicable since in truth she had been happy to exchange a big house in the west country for her father's shabby Soho flat. She went to St Paul's instead of boarding school, art galleries instead of riding to hounds. The move was supposed to be temporary, but Rachel's mother made no claim to her daughter after the split; she never settled long enough in any one place or with any one man even to think of it. She became an ever more remote voice, ringing up several days after a birthday, always mistaken in

11

Rachel's age; a hazily remembered donor of exotic presents from her travels: a blue bird from Africa, fans from Japan, a carved Indian doll from Bombay. When a friend at college showed Rachel a photograph of her in the *Tatler,* looking wonderfully elegant at a charity ball, the lovely face evoked a scent and a rustling of silks, but little more.

*   *   *

Christopher had always insisted her mother's neglect was the true source of their marital problems.

'I wish you'd read that book of Winnicott I lent you,' he would grumble. 'Of course you're damaged. If you'd ever *bothered* to go into therapy, you'd know. Never learnt how to play, that's your trouble.'

'Didn't seem to help you much,' she said.

And that was the first time Christopher hit her.

*   *   *

'Are you getting over Christopher, darling?' her mother said now, almost as if intuiting her thoughts. 'You looked so sad last time we saw each other.'

'That was my father dying,' said Rachel stiffly. 'Remember?'

'Poor Frank. Of course I remember,' said

12

her mother. 'He was always a difficult man.'

'The gentlest man in the world,' said Rachel, incensed.

'We won't argue. I used to think you were rather hard on Christopher, if it comes to that. Husbands are always difficult.'

*   *   *

Rachel took a long deep breath. 'So, who are you travelling with these days?'

'Such a charming young man. Your age, but please don't be stuffy about it. By the way, is Tom there?'

'He went to Oxford for a party,' said Rachel.

'Well, have you a number? I've a present for him.'

Rachel bit back the hope that her mother had made a sensible purchase, and read out the figures Tom had scrawled on a pad.

*   *   *

Rachel then worked all day on a review of new translations of Catullus for the TLS. The house felt peculiarly quiet; her lodgers were away. Tom was still in Oxford. She watched the television news at six without finding a single item that engaged her concern. In the early evening Christopher telephoned. He, too, it seemed, was just passing through London and was ringing about Tom.

13

'I've just lent him two hundred pounds. Is that okay? He's not going to spend it on cocaine or whatever they do these days, is he?'

'Tom doesn't do drugs,' said Rachel.

'Happen to know what he *does* want it for?'

'No idea,' said Rachel.

She was lying, because she knew very well, but it was the right answer. Christopher immediately sounded proud, male and patronising.

'Why should he bother you with his plans? Hardly a fount of common sense, are you? I gave him the money anyway.'

'Generous of you,' said Rachel with a touch of irony.

'Well, I do have another family to support,' Christopher said huffily. 'Your mother's photo was in the *Standard* yesterday. Did you see? She still looks stunning. With an actor. What's his name now . . . ?'

'I didn't notice the photo,' Rachel said.

'How does she do it? She must be pushing sixty.'

'She has good bones,' said Rachel. 'And she spends a great deal of money on herself.'

'Count your blessings, my dear,' said Christopher. 'You may not *like* having a sexy mother—daughters don't—but it's a picnic in comparison with a mother-in-law who has arthritis, I promise you.'

Rachel was furious.

'Are you suggesting I'm jealous of her?'

'Didn't say that. By the way, I don't suppose you've found a decent job yet, have you?'

'I like what I do.'

'You haven't changed a bit,' he said. 'All these years and you're still the same Rachel.'

*   *   *

And he was still the same Christopher, she reflected as he rang off. She heard his disapproval of her underprivileged, freelance life and remembered how much they had always disliked each other's style.

*   *   *

Her father had asked for Bessie Smith's 'If I Ever Get On My Feet Again' to be played as the congregation left the funeral. He had wanted his mourners to smile, whereas most had been touched to tears by the impudence. Christopher had been shocked. Yes, Christopher had been there, too; impatient, irritable, put out by the world of showbusiness that took no interest in his doings. In the fury of that difference of spirit, he and Rachel both said words so hurtful their marriage could not survive the onslaught. She did not remember all of them; her mind had been racing about in too much panic, but she could still feel the pain of Christopher's parting stab: 'You're so arrogant. Why? Where do you get that sense

15

of yourself? It must be your mother's grand relations. It's nothing you've earned.' She had not known how to reply, because something inside her was clamouring: he's right. Yes, I've read a great many books. Yes, I've brought up a clever son. But what have I done with my own talents?

*　　　*　　　*

Now the only fixed point in her life was Tom and, as a matter of fact, Rachel didn't approve of what Tom was planning in the least, but she had long ago decided to help him do whatever he wanted. She still remembered how, when she had been most alone and desolate after Christopher's departure, he had come to comfort her, no doubt with his own pain inside him, somehow older at fourteen than she was in her abandonment. He had caught her weeping in a moment of total defeat, a thin, bewildered child who found the right words to say: 'You've still got your own life. You'll be fine.' His words gave her back a sense of her own significance.

*　　　*　　　*

She remembered him as a small child going into hospital for a tonsillectomy. He had not wanted her to leave. She saw his seven-year-old face, the brave thin lips, the huge pleading

16

eyes. She had let him down then, (colluding with the nurses to have him eat anaesthetic in the form of a jelly, knowing that when she saw him the next day his throat would be raw and he would be tasting his own blood. She could still see the white face, the dark stare with which he met her treachery.

*   *   *

She could not put pressure on him to be cautious. It seemed such a miracle, even now, that Tom knew what he wanted to do and had found his own way to do it. For all his intelligence, Tom had not had an easy ride through his education. Rachel fought everyone to get him into a decent school, but still saw him sinking, out of her reach, down through the streams; a skinny, brave child, often lonely and unknown to those who were supposed to be his teachers. For a time, the disparity between his IQ and his performance in school had been so pronounced that she agreed to him seeing a therapist.

*   *   *

And then, at the age of fourteen or fifteen, everything changed. Tom discovered literature and history, sailed through examinations and won a scholarship to Balliol. She would never take that transformation for granted. It was a

17

joy of such magnitude that she held it close to her heart whenever the rest of her life went wrong. And she'd made a vow then: she would not stand in Tom's way, *whatever* he wanted to do. Christopher had often declared her adoration was unhealthy, and perhaps she did love her son too much for his own good.

*　　*　　*

Tom was nineteen, and in the last months of his gap year. Working in a bookshop and scribbling when he could, he told her. Bits and pieces. And then he'd been astonished to win a Young Journalist Award from a glossy magazine: tickets and hotel accommodation for two in Bali, plus publication of a travel piece if the editor liked what he wrote. He was going with an American school friend already up at Oxford.

*　　*　　*

Tom had been so pleased with this possibility, so full of all the things he could buy with the fee if it came through. So proud that he had found a way of using his talents. But Indonesia? She had seen the riots in May, the brutal soldiers, the truncheons, the students rolling on the floor with gas in their lungs. It demanded some courage to salute his enterprise and let him go without badgering

18

him to be careful. It was not a hugely sensible part of the world to be visiting to report on beach culture, as she had pointed out to him.

'Look on a map,' he'd told her patiently. 'Bali is a long way from Jakarta. Even further from East Timor. Nothing violent has been *happening* in Bali. At any time. The tourists still go there, for God's sake.'

*   *   *

Tom came back from Oxford in the early evening, with a large canvas holdall on his back. He was leaving in two days' time.

'Good party?' asked Rachel briskly, as if his departure gave her no anxiety whatsoever.

'It was okay. Is the catch on the drier fixed? I need to wash everything I own.'

She could see he had not yet shaved, but if he had been up all night it did not show on his face. His hair was curly as her own, but brown rather than black. It was the only resemblance he showed to Christopher, otherwise she might have been looking at a male clone of her younger self. His grey eyes were alight at the prospect of the trip.

'Are you packing tonight?' she wondered.

'I have to go into central London tomorrow, and there won't be time to do everything.'

'Had all your shots?' she enquired. 'Malaria tablets? All that kind of thing?'

'The main thing is not to get bitten by the

19

dhenge mosquitoes,' he laughed at her.

'What are you doing in town tomorrow?'

'Collecting a present from Grandmother. She's a generous old girl, isn't she?'

'In her own way,' Rachel acknowledged. 'What has she chosen, I wonder?'

'A brand new laptop.'

Rachel drew in a long breath. Tom eyed her tolerantly, amused at what she wasn't letting herself say. Then his lips opened into his widest grin.

'Don't worry, I won't defend it with my life's blood. But why don't you come with me to meet her? She said she'd like to see you.'

'I've got a deadline,' Rachel said weakly.

*   *   *

The next morning, when Tom set off for the tube, Rachel found it hard to settle. Her mother's affection for Tom was genuine enough. And Tom in turn experienced none of her mother's coldness. Was it possible that her mother could only relate easily to men?

*   *   *

All these thoughts made returning to her monitor after coffee an act of some willpower. But before she opened up her *TLS* file, she checked her email. And there, to her astonishment, was a brisk message from Ridley

Martin, suggesting 4,000 words by 10 July. Her mood lifted instantly. There were details of hotel bookings and plane tickets, and a suggestion of lunch with the celebrated Joshua Silk, evidently in Rome to oversee an Italian production of an early play. That last was enough in itself to justify her strange moment of prescience on Waterloo Bridge.

* * *

For Rachel already knew Joshua Silk. When still a child, she had stared up at him with one of those sudden, nerve-tingling crushes that beset young girls before the onset of puberty; his presence transforming even the dankest and staidest of country-house rooms into the stuff of cinema dreams. He was much the same age as the young men she was used to: those solidly built, healthy schoolboys who dressed for country pleasures, but Joshua seemed years older, being elegant and slender, with a drawn face and dark eyes. When he put his cigarette down to sit at the Tredgers' old piano, he could play any tune he was asked for, needing no music, and phrasing the words as coolly as Sinatra. He was in the Footlights at Cambridge, she knew; one of his precocious sketches had already been performed on the West End stage. He had all the forbidden allure of showbiz in a world where all that seriously counted was land and family.

21

*   *   *

Rachel watched Joshua flirting with the prettiest girls of his own age and longed to be grown up, to sidle up to him like Lauren Bacall and ask for a match, to have an electrical excitement flash between them. In the event, she hardly exchanged a word with him. It was magical enough simply to be in the same room, and hardly the less so for her mother's glaring disapproval. Those were still the Mitford years among the upper-middle classes of her mother's generation, the years of U and non-U, but somehow Joshua had bypassed the rules.

'Not even English,' her mother said, with a peculiar sniff. 'Hungarian, Czech, something like that. Awful man. I don't know why the Tredgers invite him.'

Later, when Rachel was living with her father, he'd laughed at her tentative enquiry into Joshua's origins.

'Probably Jewish,' he said. 'A *luftmensch.*'

And he'd explained the meaning of the word in Yiddish and she'd puzzled at what it would feel like to be someone who walked and lived on air, with only his wits to help him survive.

*   *   *

Joshua had left Cambridge for London by the time Rachel arrived there, and she forgot him in the odours of leaf-dust and woodsmoke, the fairytale gabled shops of Petty Cury, the joys of being young and desirable. After university she read about him from time to time in the newspapers. A play. An interview. And once, just once, in the aftermath of her break-up from Christopher, she had met him again at a party somewhere off the Portobello Road. It was the week before he won an Oscar for his screenplay *Blue Moon* and was off to LA to collect it. He had scribbled her number down but, whether he lost it or forgot her altogether, no phone call followed.

*   *   *

With her own life suddenly alive with excitement, Rachel was able to give Tom a large breakfast the next day and send him on his way to Heathrow with a coolness that surprised him. In response, he gave her a hug that lifted her from the floor.

'I'll be all right, you know,' he said. 'Don't worry. Enjoy Rome. I'll send you a fax there.'

*   *   *

Rachel boarded her own flight three days later carrying no more than a single piece of white leather hand luggage; she had learnt to travel easily and lightly. On the plane, she sat next to a cool, smartly dressed black man whose good looks were familiar. He must, she thought, be either a model or an athlete. There was a Mancunian twang to his voice as he refused the airline food and, on an impulse, because she could tell he was aware of her covert inspection, she asked him why she knew his face. He turned a slow smile in her direction and explained he was part of Britain's Olympic high-jump team. There were trials on the following day. He was a man used to women finding him sexually attractive. The eyes that met hers were amused and challenging.

'Is it *fun*? I don't mean the training, the Games themselves?'

'No.' He laughed at the idea. 'I hate the whole business.'

'I imagine there are compensations,' she said drily, wondering why he wasn't travelling in a more privileged section of the plane.

'You mean like *footballers*? No. British athletes live hand to mouth. People always think we're rich. It really pisses me off, actually.'

'I know what you mean,' she said.

Friends who remembered Rachel from the days when she spent weekends in the grand country houses of her mother's family also found it difficult to imagine she was short of money. The athlete, meanwhile, was studying her face closely.

'You on holiday?' he asked. 'Meeting someone?'

'Not exactly,' she said. 'My work sometimes takes me away from London.'

'Any children?'

'One son,' she said. 'But he's writing a travel piece, as it happens. So he's away too.'

She watched the athlete revise his notion of her age.

*   *   *

As she remembered Tom, she thought back to the novel by Emanuel Cellini, now lying in her lap. Ridley had warned her that Cellini had so far given interviews to no one, even though his book had risen to the top of the Italian bestseller lists, and gone into seven languages. He simply refused to have any social part in his success. He was in his early twenties; that much she knew, but little more. The blurb mentioned only that he had been a chess prodigy at ten. There was no photograph. She'd originally read the book in Italian, catching at the changes of voice and mood, the pervasive ache of longing, the obsessive, erotic, incoherence, but would have to read the English translation before she met him. And how was she to get to this mysterious child, this prodigy who'd made his name so precociously? She would meet Joshua Silk at the Press Club for a late lunch and he would

25

know, Ridley said, if anyone did. Rachel had no great hopes of any other outcome to their meeting. In fact she anticipated a lonely week and had already contacted the only other person she knew in Rome, Douglas Evans, a friend who worked for the British Council, who had immediately proposed she give a lecture on Seneca. She had agreed with a measure of relief. That, at least, was something she knew about.

*　　　*　　　*

At the airport, the athlete was met by a girl in yellow, her buttocks and the line between them clearly visible under her very tight short skirt. She looked little more than eighteen. For a moment or two, Rachel watched the long, perfect legs and delicate, strapped feet. Then she set off to find a taxi.

*　　　*　　　*

Her hotel was on a street between the Via Veneto and the Piazza di Spagna: cold marble, trailing plants, shining brass. At the desk, she asked if there was a fax. She was hoping Tom had acted on his promise. There was no fax.

*　　　*　　　*

She checked in, bathed and went out in the

streets, which in this part of Rome were not yet filled with tourists. It was already exceptionally hot: thirty-two degrees. In the great squares the sun could be felt like a blow on the head. She kept to the shade. Again, as at the airport, she was struck by the elegance of the women casually passing by: their well-cut short dresses, their linen suits in lime green and orange, free of the least crease, and all bespeaking another life from anything Rachel enjoyed in London. It was barely twenty minutes before she was due to meet Joshua at the Foreign Press Club.

*   *   *

Through a dark doorway, Rachel went up in the lift to the first-floor bar where she knew Joshua would be, her whole body relaxing in the relief of the air conditioning, though perhaps that was not the only reason for shivering as if with a fever. And there he was at the bar, dressed in a cool shirt and elegant Italian trousers. The years had not thickened his slender body, and his face looked even more drawn under the bone of his cheeks. For a moment she wondered if he would recognise her.

*   *   *

Joshua's eyes were as alert and watchful as a

cat's and he rose easily from the bar stool to give her a puckered kiss on the cheek.

'Shall we go through? The food is very modest here, but they do a good plate of seafood salad. What we need is a bottle of cold white wine. What are you up to? Are you here on your own?'

'Yes,' she said shortly.

* * *

She drank more of the wine than she intended, seduced by the marvellous iced chill, and began to talk a little about Tom and the perils of Indonesia. Joshua listened patiently.

'You don't need to worry about journalists,' he said. 'They don't leave the hotel bar. He'll be fine.'

Then she returned to Emanuel Cellini.

'What do you take to be the status of the novel?' she wondered. 'Is it invention or autobiography?'

'Like most fiction,' he said. 'Both. Of course that's why it's so big.'

'His father's a politician, isn't he? Giorgio Cellini. On the left. I've seen newspaper photographs of him. Rather handsome, I thought.'

He looked up from his plate to meet her eyes, and his stare embarrassed her with its directness.

'Cellini came to a party for the first night of

my play. I can repeat the usual Rome gossip about him, if you like. That dolt Ridley believes I have networking skills in any foreign city, whether I've lived there or not.'

Then his haggard face relaxed in a grin. He was cross with Ridley Martin, but wanted to help if he could.

'Tell me the gossip,' she said gently.

'Giorgio grew up on the streets after the war. An orphan. His father had been a policeman, maybe a fascist. His mother worked as a skivvy for one of the local godfathers. I don't know what happened to either of them or to any siblings. For some reason the godfather paid for Giorgio's education and sent him to university,' said Joshua, skewering a piece of octopus, 'to read law. Some say when he grew up he took over the whole operation.'

'What would *that* mean?'

'Usual stuff. Drugs, prostitution, money-laundering. Still, no one's ever brought him to book. He may be clean as a whistle.'

'I see,' said Rachel. 'What about Giorgio Cellini's wife?'

'Which one?'

'Are there several?'

'Two. The first came from a good English family, I believe. Graceful. A beauty.'

'Emanuel's mother?'

'Yes. She died when the child was about six.'

'*How* did she?'

29

'An accident. She fell from the roof terrace of the family *palazzo*. Or so they say.'

'Are you suggesting she was *pushed*?'

'No. They hint she was mentally ill. The child-genius, too, by the way. The second wife is another matter. All sorts of stories about the second Signora Cellini.'

'What kind of stories?'

'She had a very adventurous life before she married. An actress, a friend of film directors, other rich patrons.'

'Beautiful?'

'Naturally. It's not a career open to plain women.'

'And was she a good mother to Emanuel?'

'If you mean affectionate, probably. However, the marriage was annulled a few years ago.'

'On what grounds?'

'Giorgio Cellini is a very powerful figure.'

'And the child? You said he was mentally ill, but he can't have been stupid.'

'No. He was playing chess at four. Some kind of computer buff too. Disturbed is probably a better word.'

'Not surprising. It's a terrible background.'

'Oh, I don't know. There was always a huge flat on the Piazza del Popolo, a house on a lake, another in Switzerland. Mercedes cars.'

*   *   *

She could hear the anger under the ironic tone. She guessed at its source, and decided to challenge it.

'All he needed, then,' she teased him.

For a moment his face looked stony and mistrustful, but then the vertical lines in his cheeks deepened and he smiled.

'Sorry. One flabby Italian reviewer set me off. Talking about my English materialism.'

'Is that a frequent response to your plays?'

'In England I'm not often thought of as English. But this world is the only one I know. Why can't people just go on what they see? Cause and effect. History and economics.'

'And human suffering?'

'That too. The innocent go into the ovens.'

'If you are right, then none of our choices matter,' she said bleakly.

'Well, life isn't a test of anything, if that's what you mean.'

Then he saw her unhappiness.

'Is something wrong?'

'Nothing new. My father was brought up by priests, but he didn't want me taught by them. I don't know what I do believe. Sometimes nothing at all.'

Rachel had been determined to be businesslike. Practical. Instead she found herself saying, 'I used to wonder . . . What took you to the Tredgers'.'

'What interested them in me, you mean,' he corrected her, unabashed. 'You're quite right, of course—it does need an explanation. Fortunately it's an easy one. When we were at school together they discovered my uncle knew pop stars.'

Her blue eyes opened wide.

'*How* did he?'

'Used to own a club in Soho. I took the Tredgers to a party where they could goggle at John Lennon.'

'And did you keep up with them? Afterwards?'

'If you mean the Tredgers, I was all the rage for a time at Trinity. Lots of country weekend shoots. If you mean the Beatles et al., on the other hand—' Joshua's face creased wryly. 'I never saw them again. My uncle sold the club. At a great loss.'

He filled up their glasses with the last of the wine, and she accepted willingly. She was enjoying herself, but rather under false pretences, she thought, saying as much without pausing for reflection.

'No. No.' He reached forward, patting her hand. 'I can do *something*. If not as much as Ridley imagines. For instance, I can get you to see Papa Cellini. He'll be having supper tonight with an old friend of mine. I've already spoken to her, and she'll be delighted to invite you.'

'Which friend is that?'

'Anna Carey that used to be. She's married to the present English ambassador, Sir Peter

Forrest.'

'*Is* she?' said Rachel, without enthusiasm. 'She was a year or two ahead of me at Cambridge. Didn't she become a model?'

'For a time. And then she made a "good" marriage. She enjoys the social world here.'

'Why is our Embassy spending money on the entertainment of gangsters?' Rachel asked, with a glint in her eye.

'Because Giorgio Cellini is also a leading politician. In the running for high office, by the way. And the party isn't in his honour. It's to welcome Ezekiel Stern.'

'The American critic? Of course I'd like to go.'

'I wish I'd read your father's novels more recently,' said Joshua after a pause.

'I think they are all out of print now.'

'Fashions change. It's what newspapers do.'

'A *luftmensch*,' she said softly.

He looked startled to hear the word on her lips and she could see he was also a little hurt. She hastened to explain how she had learnt the word, that her father meant no harm by it, that he had in mind something magical, a kind of conjuring out of the air. Joshua looked mollified but doubtful.

'It is the word my relations would use for confidence tricksters and cheats,' he pointed out. 'People who don't have a trade.' Then, to her delight, his dark face broke open into a laugh. 'Fair enough. What better place than the theatre for people who live on air?'

*   *   *

The bathroom in the Foreign Press Club, tiled blue and white, was blessedly clean and cool. For a time Rachel sat there moodily. It was a long time since she had felt sexually alive. It distracted her from her present quest. She tried to remember who it was Joshua had married. An actress, she thought glumly. Or was it another model? She would not let herself wonder if they were still together.

*   *   *

When she went back to the table, Joshua seemed uneasy himself.

'You be careful,' he warned her, almost as she would have liked to speak to her son Tom.

'Of what?'

'Cellini. You'll fall for him, I shouldn't wonder.'

'He must be an old man,' she said, startled. 'And it's the son I'm interested in, surely, not the father. What's worrying you?'

'Women like you always fall for thugs,' he said moodily.

'Women like me?'

He was looking at her very intently.

'Intelligent women,' he said. 'With ambitions.'

34

* * *

She wondered how much he knew about her, tried to remember what she might have talked about the last time they met. Christopher, probably. Had Christopher been a thug? Of course he had in his way. And more temporary partners? Her married lover had been gentle enough, but his need for her had been intermittent at first and, when at last he was ready to make himself altogether available, she had mysteriously lost interest. And what about Joshua himself, if it came to that? She was charmed by him, but nothing in his manner suggested reliability.

* * *

'Playing sleuth is dangerous,' he warned her.

'I'll go back to the hotel,' she said. 'I'm going to read the Cellini novel again in English. Does that sound safe enough for you?'

Joshua wrote the address of the Ambassador's personal residence on a sheet of paper for her, and made a note of her telephone number.

'I'll stay in touch,' he promised.

* * *

35

Back in the hotel, Rachel went up to her bedroom and turned on CNN. Not much new and nothing about Indonesia, she was relieved to see. She undressed and propped herself naked against the pillows, her legs bent up and the television screen visible through them. Then she began to read. It was a hot June afternoon and the air conditioning was more noisy than effective. Rachel lay back, her legs falling open to show the thick black hair between them, the noise of the TV pattering along as she read. She wasn't sleepy. The book itself continued to trouble her with its hints of strange passions: an incestuous love between a son and his stepmother, with suggestions of paedophilia, too, since the boy seemed barely to have reached puberty. It was written in many voices but it began through the eyes of an anxious child whose life had been one long experience of loss and betrayal.

CHAPTER TWO

At first there was only softness, a smell of sweet linen and gentle hands; her smell, her hands. Body warmth. Safety. Then, standing behind the wooden bars of the cot and shouting for her. A long wordless wail, answered by other faces, voices in another language, nothing that reached the ache of his need. As if the fat jolly woman who soaped him in warm water could ease that longing. When she came at last to bend over him and put him comfortably on his pillow, he would not settle, wanting to be held, to put his head into her neck, to feel his tears on her skin. To be assured she would never leave again. He learned to pull at her thick golden hair, refusing to give up his hold, not wanting to hurt but to keep her close while she kissed his fingers and tried to disengage them. But at last he always lost his grip, and then there was only warm milk to soothe him into sleep.

*　　　*　　　*

—Will you stop crying, a boy of your age, crying like that, what is it now?

　—He doesn't know what he wants.

　—He wants to go outside.

　—It's too hot. It's a heatwave. Just be quiet. Ignore him.

　—Is the doctor still here?

　—He went an hour ago.

　—How is she?

　—I can't tell you any more in front of the boy.

　—He understands nothing. Look at him.

*　　　*　　　*

When was it? He was alone on white sands

with her, the green water under their toes, lapping round their feet in gentle waves. She put cream on his skin which was white as her own, adjusted the coloured parasol to protect them from the sun, lay back on a towel while he played with his ball.

—Ball, she said. Where is the ball?

And he found it for her.

—Book? Where is the book?

And she applauded him.

—Good boy. Clever boy.

* * *

In her language he could read.

In her language he could speak.

* * *

But were they alone? Sometimes, he remembered a strong swimmer coming out of the sea to laugh at their side. To carry him shrieking out of his depth and hold him high in the air. It must have been his father, lean and brown-skinned and unafraid of the sun's strength.

* * *

Whenever his father came home, he was taken away by other hands, however much he wriggled and held out his arms towards her.

38

Put back in his own room. There was a cold bed and moonlight from the garden, and his night clothes wet. He remembered tears and anger. He could climb out by then, and crawl to the top of the stairs and hear the two of them far below. Or rather his father's voice, her tender words too low to make out, the other, deeper growl flowing over hers like a river. All the other voices, as he grew older, were stronger than hers.

*   *   *

She gave him books, and he learned the words of her language and their shapes on the page. It seemed as if he had always known them, always understood the signs that spoke in her voice. It was their secret. But she was tired and pale and his father said teaching was too much for her. So then there was a priest who taught him Italian words, his father's language, with his father's resonant melody in it. He made it out on the page easily enough, he made the signs of it with his pen as elegantly as anyone could desire. Why should he speak in it? His mother's language was the one he spoke in; he had learnt it on her lap, when he was still allowed to sit there peacefully. Before. Before whatever happened. If he could remember that.

*   *   *

When did the two strong men lift him off the bed and carry him gagging on a rag down the stairs? He could still taste the fluff of the blanket. When was he bundled into the boot of that car? He could hear the heavy lid close tight over him like a steel coffin. Then the quiet engine began to purr and the gates of the garden opened. Someone in the house had wanted him out of the way, that was obvious. They were stealing him away from her and what hurt most was not his own fear but the thought of her terror when she woke the next morning and looked for him. As he imagined her grief there were tears in his nose and snot in his throat until he began retching into the blanket and the car pulled over to the kerb.

—Basta, basta, a voice said, gently enough.

They did not want him dead in his own vomit.

It came through to him that they did not want him dead.

But still the tears came. How would she bear it?

* * *

Before that. Before that. At night, she would stand and watch for the stars where they hung in the night sky. She named them for him.

—You cannot see the stars in Rome, she had whispered. The lights of the city extinguish their power. Here in the countryside you can see them as they were in the ancient world.

*   *   *

And she taught him where to find the Plough and the Pleiades and told him the stories of the ancient myths, and he had listened and loved her more than the stars and more than the Gods they immortalised. Did she stand on her balcony alone now to enjoy the skies? He could not believe she wanted to be imprisoned in her room away from him. And she was alone whenever his father was away.

*   *   *

He could not believe she had ordered him away from her, that she had chosen the separation. Though they tried to explain it was so. She lay in her room with the balcony over the gardens, her meals taken in on a tray. He could see her in pale green silk, her drawn face against white pillows, the light breezes of summer coming through the window with the scents of the trees.

*   *   *

She was ill, he knew she was ill, and he found a silver bell, in the shape of a Victorian lady in a crinoline, so she could ring it easily if she didn't have the breath to call out and he'd come running to her bedside. But now he sometimes woke in the night and heard the tinkling sound in his ears, or dreamed he did and cried. Not for himself, but because she was alone. And sometimes he could hear his father laughing downstairs with his friends just as if nothing were happening to her.

*   *   *

It was a house of marble floors and walls hung with paintings of men and women in rich clothes. He liked to stare at the thick paint and see it first as fur and diamond and then as flecks of pigment. Once he crept down the first stairs of the curving staircase to listen.

*   *   *

—Don't move away when I'm talking to you.

That was his father's voice. From the atrium perhaps, or the library, where the door stood open. Or was it from the room that opened to the garden, the room with her painting in it, looking like a child herself? Then the words muffled. Her soft voice in Italian. Then the deep voice on and on so that he could drown in it.

*   *   *

—You don't think. You feel, but you don't think. Do you? Your family, with their English parks, and their shallow ideas, what do they know about me?

*　　　*　　　*

Then murmurs, scuffles. Her cry of pain. Or he thought it was pain. And his father's voice again, gentler now. Mysteriously softened.

*　　　*　　　*

—I'm incurable . . . I'm too old to change . . . I'm a shit . . . Forgive me.

*　　　*　　　*

Of one thing at least the boy was sure. *He* would never forgive his father. Never try to understand him. Whatever he explained.

*　　　*　　　*

When was it, when? She would stroke his hair, and speak as if to herself in a low voice.

*　　　*　　　*

—Don't be hurt, little one. Your father can trust no one. He thinks you are pretending.

43

That you are silent out of malice. Last night he woke me in the night to tell me that, and I tried to soothe him. But it doesn't matter. I can do no more here. We'll go away to Scotland. Let's lie and think of the silver water and the brightness. Sunshine without this terrible Roman heat. Will you come home with me?

*   *   *

He would go anywhere with her. If only she would go. But she only dreamed of it. They went nowhere. He didn't try to remind her or ask her if she had forgotten. Sometimes she took him out on the terrace in the blue moonlight, to hear the owls. He had an inkling then of something that held her, a puzzling cord that tugged at her heart.

*   *   *

—Why do those birds hoot so loudly? he wondered. When the sound must alert their prey.

—They cry to one another, she told him. They love one another. Even birds of prey must love and find a mate.

—Then there were tears on her face and, though he kissed them away, he knew her thoughts had wandered far away from him, and his love no longer reached her. His father

44

had gone away and she grieved at his absence.

*   *   *

Everyone else had a little world inside their head, behind the eyes; separate, strange, unreachable. Unguessable. How could anyone tell what someone else was doing in their mind? Nobody knew. They thought they did, but they were guessing. As he guessed her feelings, sometimes believing her thoughts were inside him even as she conceived them, as if the two of them made one continuous being, connected by the same bloodstream, as they must once have been.

*   *   *

The priest says God sees everything, even though he says nothing. But who knows about God? If there is a God. The boy wondered: did God see the black-haired servant girl in her green dress that shimmered with sequins? Did he see the woman with red hair who came late at night and laughed as she climbed upstairs on his father's arm?

*   *   *

When his father set out the chess board and asked him, Shall we play chess? he always nodded for an answer. Why should he speak to this enemy? It pleased him to defeat the man so easily. He liked to listen to him breathing heavily as he moved his pieces, to predict his play and find a way through.

*   *   *

—You have learnt the moves so well, his father would mutter. The doctors know nothing. You have a remarkable intelligence. Why don't they see that?

And the boy laughed. How could he have explained it, the difference between the blessed world of the board where there were rules, and the bewildering world of people where there were none. People could do anything. Cry and shout and hit one another. Everything was so violent and unpredictable, how could the ordinary girls in the kitchen or the gardeners' boys cope with such terror? They were the remarkable ones. What he could do was so much simpler. Why could no one else see as quickly as he did the shapes unfolding ahead, one after another, as fast as blips on a screen?

*   *   *

No one could read the human world of events ahead. They might think they could, but it was impossible. He knew now. First he learnt to bear the loneliness of separations. And then

46

she stayed altogether in her room, while he sat on the terracotta flags under the kitchen table. To listen and guess. There was so much he could no longer put in sequence.

*   *   *

—But how could it happen?

—Will you be quiet! Who knows what goes on in his mind?

—Let him have one of the cakes if he wants it.

—Will you take him away?

—The family arrives soon.

—I think they are already downstairs.

—They'll be talking to the doctor.

—Their grief must be terrible.

—And the other one?

—What are you saying?

—You know what I'm saying.

—Will you stop! She isn't here.

—She stayed last night. You know she wears red knickers? I saw them.

—Hush now. The boy is listening. You can see he's listening. Little one? Do you want a biscuit, darling?

—The way that child looks at you. Like he knows everything in the world only he isn't saying.

—He ordered figs after the meal last night and his usual sweet wine. Nothing touches him.

—Be quiet. The child is trying to speak.

—Bend down and listen.

—I can make no sense of it.

*   *   *

There was so much he had forgotten. When was it he had lain in his own bed, with pain tormenting him, and the doctors indifferent, and only her figure to soothe him? Not that her caress helped or assuaged the burning ache inside. When he thought about those weeks of delirium he could not even bring her face clearly to mind: the grey eyes seemed greener, the pale cheeks more toughly boned, the soft hands browner and less delicate. Sometimes he doubted the memory. All he knew was that he had been ill, and when he came through that illness, she was gone.

CHAPTER THREE

As Rachel's taxi arrived at the residence of the British Ambassador in the San Giovanni district about a quarter of an hour before she was expected, she was conscious of an enjoyable quickening of her pulse rate, which made her hesitate after paying the driver. The mirror of her elegant pewter compact showed her face perfectly cool, her eyes clear, her skin free of perspiration. She was enjoying the role of detective.

*   *   *

Behind the railings lay a long path beneath cedar trees. Even as she mused, the taxi drove off impatiently and the guard, accompanied by a large black dog, approached the gate. The animal began to bark, perhaps surprised to see her on foot since cars, she guessed, would usually drive up to deposit their passengers at the doors of the Ambassador's mansion. She smiled at the gatekeeper. It was all right. Her name was on the list of those expected.

'I'm early,' she explained.

He responded at once to her voice, the voice of someone who had spent her childhood in houses grand enough to make this one no more than mildly imposing. He gave her friendly directions about the path through the gardens.

*   *   *

There was a loud chirruping of Mediterranean night sounds. The black dog walked quietly beside her as she took the path uphill under the trees, until the flat stones turned sharply to the left and she found herself at the door of the ambassadorial residence, the yellow walls glowing in the last of the sun. And there stood

49

Lady Anna to greet her: a woman of about six foot; her broad face handsome, her hair somewhere between blonde and early grey, thick and well cut. She was still a handsome woman, though perhaps less pretty than Rachel remembered her. Her bearing was formidable, and everything about her exuded a marvellous confidence.

'Honestly, Rachel,' she exclaimed. 'Why didn't the taxi bring you up to the house?'

'The man was in a hurry. Doesn't matter. I walked up with your dog.'

'In this heat? How quaint,' said Anna.

She was placid enough about eccentricity, though her eyes scanning Rachel were looking for something else.

'You look cool enough. Like your mother. She could wear a silk scarf pinned with a paperclip and people always thought it was Versace. How is she these days?'

'She passed through London a little while back.'

'She must be the most tremendous fun. We used to giggle over her escapades in the nursery. She always came to visit with a different man.'

'Did she?'

'You weren't close, I suppose. Well. I hope the dog didn't trouble you.'

Rachel patted the black head amiably.

'I don't usually take to Rottweilers,' she said. 'But this one seems very friendly.'

*   *   *

The two women were much of an age, and inevitably their eyes assessed one another, perhaps speculating about such very different lives. Rachel observed the English skin, the air of comfortable country privilege. Yet, even as Rachel admired Lady Anna's carriage, her poise and the style in which she lived, she felt no envy. She's done nothing remarkable, she thought. She lives here grandly; she's married successfully but she's done even less than I have.

'You're looking rather well,' said Lady Anna, completing her scrutiny of Rachel's dark silk dress, bought that morning near the Piazza di Spagna on a Barclaycard.

Rachel murmured something polite, as Lady Anna led them into the ambassadorial entrance hall.

'I was surprised to hear Joshua Silk was still in Rome,' Lady Anna said. 'His play is doing quite well enough without his presence, I'd have thought. And he never stays *anywhere* without some kind of reason.'

'He said something about his family,' said Rachel demurely. She had wondered as much herself.

'Come on, he doesn't have any family. All dead,' said Lady Anna. 'If you don't know that, you don't know him very well.'

'I don't,' said Rachel.

'No? Well, don't tell me if you don't want to. Anyway, he isn't here tonight.'

*   *   *

'Living in this house must be quite demanding,' Rachel said, glancing into a room the size of a ballroom.

'Luckily we have a flat on the top floor. We don't have to bother with the other rooms, except for official occasions. We're eating on the terrace tonight.'

Rachel followed her hostess up the stairs.

*   *   *

The terrace was wide and floored in yellow stone; it overlooked a garden filled with poplars and birch trees, from which smells of jasmine and honeysuckle rose alluringly. There was a gleaming white table set with silver and plates but not yet covered with food. Sir Peter Forrest, a very good-looking, well-bred Englishman, was at that moment on his knees, lighting tapers of mosquito repellent. There were rewards, Rachel reflected, in sustaining a long relationship. She wondered whether Sir Peter had been faithful to his downright, laughing wife, or whether she allowed him an open marriage. When Sir Peter looked up to greet her, Rachel saw at once in his hot blue eyes how much he enjoycd an adventurous life. For a moment she was angry for Anna. And then she gave a little shrug. It was how things were now. It was how the world had always been in the English upper classes. She responded coolly.

*   *   *

The guest of honour was still in his room after a transatlantic flight, but other guests had begun to arrive and were offered drinks by Embassy servants. They seemed to know one another: diplomats, local dignitaries, wives as spruce as models, Italian literary figures, perhaps particularly requested by the distinguished guest. Rachel knew she could pass with ease among the white shoulders bare to the waist, the black tubes of dresses that must have cost a Roman fortune, and still feel assured; even though she had long since dropped out of this privileged world. I'm neither in this world nor out of it, thought Rachel. I'm at the edges, I've always been at the edges.

'And where is there a finer place?' her father's Irish growl mocked her. 'Where's the centre now? There was a time when England had an Empire and London was the heart of it. Not these days. Where would English literature be without the immigrants?'

*   *   *

As she made her way round the terrace, there was talk of poetry, Cambridge and her British Council lecture. The conversation was polite, but unmemorable. Rachel spoke when she was spoken to, but made no attempt to penetrate the tight, inturned groups.

*   *   *

Suddenly she became aware of the arrival of a handsome, bitter-faced man, for whom the other groups parted uneasily. She knew at once this must be Giorgio Cellini. She had seen his face in newspaper photographs, of course, but they gave no sense of his presence in the flesh. He was tall, impeccably dressed in a light grey suit, perhaps silk, certainly handmade; with granite good looks and an unmistakable sexual magnetism: something in the slant of his face as he smiled, something that created a kind of fluttering in the women around him, even Lady Anna. Rachel held herself a little aloof, unwilling to be part of such a dovecote, and a little irritated with Joshua for assuming she would succumb with the others. Yet there was no sense in being at the party if she could not make some contact with the man. He's old enough to find me young, she thought.

*   *   *

When Rachel was introduced to him, Cellini's eyes went over her trim body, guessing perhaps at her availability. She smiled back into his eyes and then withdrew a little. She was not without cunning in these matters. Even as she moved and laughed, she could feel his attention follow her.

*   *   *

Now the guest of honour had arrived: a short, flat-faced man with colourless eyes and a slightly awkward body. Without raising his voice, and with no apparent effort, he gathered the room around him with a social magnetism quite unlike Cellini's. She had heard Stern lecture: he liked to speak without notes, compelling the audience with sentences that seemed to spring perfectly formed to his lips. There were those who disliked him. Or envied him. But she admired his work. Only Cellini held himself apart, a little stiffly, though he too listened, she observed.

*   *   *

'When I was twelve or so my father brought me a tutor. He wanted me to go to Harvard. The tutor taught me for a while and then said, "Don't you think you should consider adopting

55

another name? Ezekiel? Think about it. The boys will tease you." "Then they will find reasons to tease me anyway," I replied. "It would be much better to go to the University of Los Angeles." So I did.'

*   *   *

A voice from the crowd asked him about TS Eliot, whose alleged anti-Semitism had that year made a stir in the liberal English press.

'The question is much larger,' Stern began, a gleam in his eye. 'Larger even than the question of Céline and Maurras . . .'

And, as his audience listened, hypnotised, he launched into an analysis of that strange mixture of intelligence and evil so often, as he believed, mingled at the root of human genius. Rachel found this disquisition so fascinating that for some moments she was unaware that Giorgio Cellini had moved to station himself at her side.

*   *   *

When she felt his presence, she repressed a little start and, remembering the evening's purpose, gave him her full attention.

'What is it you are here to do in Rome?' he asked.

There was a sexual curiosity in his face, but something else too.

56

'I am here to give a lecture to the British Council. On Seneca.'

'So. You are an academic woman?' He was surprised but a little intrigued, she could see.

'You don't like intellectual woman?' she guessed, her eyes dancing.

'Every woman has her own cleverness,' he said, his eyes very intently on her face. 'But I know more than you think. You are also a journalist, isn't that so?'

She did not drop her blue flirtatious gaze but she was alarmed.

'Who told you that?'

'Before I come to such an evening, I check who will be here.'

'I'm only a *literary* journalist,' she stressed.

'So you have no interest in my political opinions?'

'Only if you want to tell me about them,' she said.

*   *   *

For a moment the flow of conversation was checked and Rachel was glad to overhear some talk of the latest film to come out of America.

'You enjoy such films?' Cellini asked her.

She shook her head vehemently.

'The ordinary world seems scary enough. Why would *anyone* want to sit in the dark and watch other people torturing one another?'

He looked amused by her indignation.

'The pleasures of the voyeur, naturally. Men like to see someone else blowing off the head of a bank manager. Young men even giggle. Tarantino understands all that. It's a game. Not like a battlefield, or a casualty ward, where most of them would be sick in two minutes.'

'Maybe men enjoy these films more than women.'

'Women take a different kind of pleasure in violence,' he smiled.

'Men like to believe that,' she exclaimed.

'So no woman could enjoy being raped?'

'Certainly not.'

'Some enjoy the fantasy, however.'

The voice of Ezekiel was rising again over the crowd. He had finished his peroration.

'It is not only the torturer who takes pleasure in pain,' he was concluding.

'You seem to have some support,' Rachel said, a little shakily.

*   *   *

The waiters were setting out dinner, and she collected her plate and helped herself to the delicious purée of vegetables, the fish *en croute,* the salad of fresh asparagus.

When Ezekiel Stern was introduced, he claimed to know her already.

'You were still an undergraduate when I was

at Cambridge for a year,' he said, bowing over her hand. 'I admired you. Only at a distance, naturally.'

*   *   *

She was flattered, and let him hold her hand a little longer than was entirely proper.

'Have you seen the Coliseum?' he demanded, his pale eyes gleaming. 'They are rebuilding it.'

She confessed she had not yet done so.

'There is nothing else in Europe to equal such an *immense* undertaking,' Stern declared. 'Rome was the first modern city.' It was a topic which seemed to fill him with enthusiasm. 'The imitations have not been beautiful. Think of Vienna. Of Berlin. All those cities aping Roman greatness.'

'But what will they use the building for? A sports stadium?'

'Nothing so banal, I hope.'

'Perhaps the games played by Imperial Rome?' she teased.

She could feel Cellini watching her, gauging the response she elicited from the Great Man.

'Rome is a licentious city. Always was,' said Stern. 'Christianity did not conquer Rome, Rome conquered Christianity. Did you know the games went on for a hundred years after Constantine?'

*   *   *

Cellini joined her again when Stern was led away to be presented to a more important guest.

We were talking about the Coliseum,' she said, feeling the need to have some palpable content to a conversation which had become heavily charged with an unspoken excitement. Cellini was attracted to her; it was unmistakable. And she recognised the quality of her own inner disturbance. Damn, she thought. How disgusting women are. It must be something in the genetic make-up, too commonplace to be a perversion, this sexual attraction towards power without the least concern for morality.

'It's important commercially,' he said indifferently. Tell me, are you only squeamish about violence?'

For the first time she made out the hint of an Italian accent.

'Have you looked at our newly discovered frescoes?'

'I've read about them,' she said slowly.

She knew these were pornographic images. Men with men, sometimes one man with two women. Men copulating with donkeys.

'For the bath houses of our ancient aristocracy,' he said, as if challenging her to be prudish.

'What gives people pleasure,' she began, 'is

60

different.'

'Don't you have to ask—who is taking the pleasure?' he shrugged. 'The woman with a penis down her throat? The slave with a whip in his arse?'

His voice remained matter-of-fact.

'I'm not interested in a sensuality which is so impersonal,' she said, conscious that her words ran across his and answered a question which had never been put, though he did not react as if her reply were at a tangent.

'So, you are looking for simple, unsophisticated love?'

'If I were looking for any,' she said, flushing.

*   *   *

To break the sense of danger that had begun to enclose her, she began to talk rapidly. About Seneca, Euripides, Nero, the imagery of the games, the prostitutes waiting outside the Coliseum to assuage the desires aroused by bloodshed. And suddenly became aware that the party was coming to an end, without any move on her part to find out anything about this man's son.

'How are you getting back to your hotel?' he asked her.

'A taxi, I suppose.'

'Let me offer you a lift in my car. It will collect me here in ten minutes.'

For a moment Joshua's face came vividly

into her mind, but she dismissed his warning and accepted. Then she said:

'I very much admired your son's novel.'

The dark face did not alter its expression, but she could feel the quality of his attention change completely.

'People do,' he said. 'I understand.'

'I would very much like to meet him. To write about him. He is a puzzle. So young, and so talented.'

'He does as he likes. Ask him.'

'I don't have his phone number.'

'Ask his publisher.'

'They say he changes it every week,' she said. 'For your own part, were you surprised by the book's success?'

'Nothing Emanuel does would surprise me,' he said, after a pause.

She met his eyes with her bluest and most impudent stare, and found that his had become hostile. It was unmistakable: this man hated his son passionately.

*   *   *

The manner of Rachel's leaving made a strange contrast to her manner of arrival. The car was a white Mercedes, the chauffeur uniformed and subservient. Even before the car moved, the interior was chilled with air conditioning.

'Is it too much?' Cellini asked her. 'The cold

air?'

'No. It's heaven,' she said.

She had crossed her legs so that her skirt rode up rather high and she could feel the suede on her thighs.

*   *   *

If Cellini were still excited by her propinquity, he gave no further sign of it. It was as if Rachel's mention of his son had diverted him away from any libidinous thought. He talked instead about the role of the Church in Italian society. He was eloquent about those who gloated at the collapse of Eastern Europe, as though God had made his will manifest through the victory of capitalism.

'The rich like to pretend the free market has something to do with liberty. All it means is the freedom for the poor to starve in the world's gutters,' he concluded bitterly.

Rachel found no ready reply. As a detective, she thought crossly, she was not proving a great success.

*   *   *

As she fell silent, it seemed to her that the presence of Giorgio Cellini had subtly changed its quality. He was displeased, she decided. And when displeased, he seemed more alarming.

63

'The Church made only one correct diagnosis. Women and men have different affections, and satisfy themselves in very different ways. To be blessed as a woman is to be a mother happy in her children,' Cellini was saying. 'Do you have children?'

'I have a son,' she said, a little flicker of superstitious terror touching her as she spoke, as if it were unlucky.

*   *   *

When the car arrived at her hotel, the driver helped her circumspectly out of the car and she hurried in shivering, perhaps from the chill of the car. Glancing back, she saw Cellini lean forward to give directions. He looked again as she had first seen him: a heavy man of sixty years in formal dress. He was travelling back into his own life. As she watched the car move off, she admitted to herself for the first time that the encounter had frightened her and that she was relieved to see him go.

*   *   *

The spectacled man behind the desk nodded to her and, before she asked, pointed to the empty pigeonhole under her room number. There was no message, no fax. She had a moment of serious unease about Tom, which she did her best to quash.

As she travelled up in the lift, she reminded herself that many of her own forebears had taken far greater risks. Younger sons on her mother's side of the family, having no hope of the parental estate, had charted unknown tribes and explored jungles. They would be out of touch with home for months or years, not days. Some, at Tom's age, had gone out into the farthest parts of the Empire to rule absurdly vast tracts of land. If their mothers were nervous, they had put up with it.

*   *   *

She shrugged off the anxiety as ignoble, but she found herself unable to relax. She felt let down, disappointed. Angry with herself because she had learnt so little. When she reached her room she decided she must put her British Council talk in order and plan a little sightseeing for the morning.

*   *   *

The telephone rang as she fumbled the card key into the lock.

'Rachel? You're back. That's good. What happened?'

'*Joshua!*' She paused. 'Nothing very much.'

65

'You mean Cellini didn't show up?'

'Yes, he was there. But I muffed it completely. We talked about Roman licentiousness and contemporary film and he brought me back to the hotel in his car. But I'm no nearer to the son.'

'Listen,' he said, 'it's only ten-thirty. You can't go to sleep yet.'

'But I still have the rest of the Cellini book to read,' said Rachel.

'You could do that perfectly well in the morning,' he pointed out. After a moment's pause, he asked, 'Did you fancy Cellini?'

She hesitated.

'I thought as much. Now, I've been thinking. Why do you suppose Emanuel is so determined to stay hidden?'

'I suppose he's avoiding people like me. Must be a kind of shyness.'

'It's a bit extreme, though, isn't it? Have you ever wondered whether he has something to *hide*?'

'Family secrets, you mean? I wouldn't have thought so. I mean, the novel is hardly reticent.'

'It's just a hunch I have. Maybe he has good reason to be frightened. Giorgio Cellini seems to scare a good many people. Why should his son be any different?'

'The boy certainly doesn't come across as a macho figure,' she admitted. 'Have you found anyone who knows him?'

'Yes. Would you like to look in on a kitsch little nightclub? Art deco lamps and quite a good singer, if I can tempt you.'

'I'll be right down when I've cleaned up a bit.'

'You don't need to change,' said Joshua reflectively. 'I watched you go in.'

'*How* did you?'

'I'm parked across the street. An odd thing, though. I have a feeling I'm not the only person to take an interest in your movements. Listen, I have a suggestion. I'll drive round to the back of the hotel. You go down in the lift and walk out into the courtyard. I'll be there.'

'Are you sure all that's really necessary?'

'Yes. You're being followed.'

        *   *   *

She thought about Joshua's last remark as she ducked out of the fire door in the lobby. She didn't believe anyone would find it worth having her tailed, and something in her didn't quite trust Joshua, for all his helpfulness. Or perhaps because of it.

        *   *   *

Joshua was driving a red Peugeot, which he was finding too small for him. As Rachel got in and shut the door, he shuffled his seat further backwards, the better to accommodate his legs. When he started the engine, the gearbox growled in protest, but he backed out adroitly enough.

'Bloody hired car. Why don't Italians like automatic gears?'

'Let's hope we don't get into some melodramatic car chase,' she murmured. 'Where are we making for?'

'I know somewhere we can park and then walk.'

*   *   *

The moon was very full. They were driving along a great oval piazza, which she recognised from earlier in the day. There was a huge Bernini statue at its heart.

*   *   *

Joshua paused for a moment before deciding which way to turn.

'They used to torture heretics here, long ago,' he said conversationally. 'The poor sods ran round this oval for the amusement of the local citizens. They were whipped, and sometimes burnt, here.'

'I thought it was where they held chariot races,' she said, startled. That's what it says in the guide book.'

'Heretics for burning,' he assured her. 'Ah, here we are. We can leave the car and walk.

68

It's not too far.'

*   *   *

The thud of a car door and a shouted word of farewell sounded hollow in the hot night air. He led her alongside the scaffolding and polythene which covered a church in the process of restoration.

*   *   *

'Down here,' he said, after they'd turned a series of corners. 'Where the lights are. If you're still game.'

He put out his hand and smiled, and she held on tightly as she climbed down the curving iron stairs into a smoke-filled underground restaurant. From below came the beat of American pop music.

*   *   *

At one wall stood a grand piano which was far too large for the room. As they took their seats at a table already reserved for them, the singer took her place on a stool at the side of the piano. She had a bright, wide-lipped mouth, blonde hair and eyes that glittered when she opened them wide. She was dressed in a black velvet coat, under which Rachel glimpsed red and purple. When she had finished her first song—a piece of sentimental pop—she unbuttoned the coat, smiled at the pianist and began singing a Billie Holiday classic, with her own contemporary variation.

*   *   *

'She's surprisingly good,' said Rachel.

The singer had a strong, deep voice, and every gesture of her hand and every angle of her face was styled to perfection. At the end of the number, she threw her coat carelessly on the floor and Rachel could make out tiny straps, strong shoulders and dense purple sequins over the breasts. The dress was cut to the thighs, but the fishnet stockings only showed when the singer sat on a stool and let the material of her dress fall between her legs.

'*Very* good,' Rachel murmured.

'Right both times. Except she isn't a she. She's Danni Alloni. He was in a show of mine a couple of years ago.'

'Transvestite?' Rachel was incredulous. 'Or some kind of sex change?'

'As to that . . .' Joshua shrugged. 'Some of them have the operation in Singapore, some of them are tarting around while they're saving up for it.'

*   *   *

Joshua took a card from his pocket and gave it

70

to a waitress. 'Nothing here is quite as it seems,' said Joshua. 'This was always a theatre haunt. You see that guy over there, in braces with a blue shirt? He's one of the last great clowns. Fellini used him.'

*   *   *

The pop music had begun again, blasting through the small room, and destroying all possibility of conversation. Rachel looked down at the menu, which offered cocktails with American names.

'What are we *doing* here?' she mouthed to Joshua.

He bent towards her.

'We're here to talk to the star. He owns the place, by the way.'

'Why would we do *that*?' she asked.

'Because he knows Emanuel Cellini.'

She looked sceptical.

'Yes,' he insisted. 'I promise. Alloni used to earn a crust as a private tutor. When he was young and unemployed. He taught the boy composition.'

'*Really?*' She made no attempt to disguise her incredulity.

'Do try and remember he looks perfectly respectable in a suit.'

*   *   *

And then Danni himself was at the table, larger than he had seemed by the piano and, for all the flirtatious toss of his head, decidedly less female. An aroma of breath-sweetening cachous wafted from him as he spoke. Both his eyelids and his upper cheekbones were daubed with glitter.

'Hello, gorgeous,' he said to Joshua. 'I heard you were here. Couldn't believe my luck. You've always been such a *tease.*' He snapped a finger at one of the waitresses. 'Let's have champagne. He's such a wicked boy, isn't he?' he confided to Rachel. 'You never know *what* he's after.'

Rachel, out of her depth, could find nothing to say.

'Why can't you lower the volume of that damned music?' frowned Joshua.

'The punters like it. No one can guess a word, so they don't have to be shy. No one can listen to what we're saying, either. So now— what was it you wanted to talk to me about, Joshua darling?'

*   *   *

Rachel stared from one to the other, helplessly. Joshua said something she couldn't hear and Danni, smiling, put out his tongue as a reply. It was a narrow flick of a tongue, like a snake's, thought Rachel, trying to read his lips. Then suddenly there was no problem making out the words.

'Sorry, sweetheart, can't help there. I was warned off talking to you at all, if you want to know. But I said to myself, maybe he's looking for a drag queen. He's the big time, and I'm greedy. So okay, I made a mistake. Here's the champagne. Have a drink on me and then fuck off out of here.'

'Someone warned you? Who warned you?' asked Joshua.

'None of your business.'

'A natural question, though.'

'Why would I answer any pain-in-the-arse questions?' said Danni. 'Perhaps I'm not making myself clear. Here in this club I have— what do you call it?—a nice little earner. And I'm not looking for trouble.' He stood up. 'Take a tip from me, Joshua baby. Don't—'

*   *   *

And then, just as the image of his glittering body towered above them, the lights in the whole building went out. As if in freeze frame, Rachel caught the outline of Joshua's face as he seized her hand. The music had stopped abruptly, and there were confused cries and a few giggles. Then, in the darkness, these sounds were replaced by loud whistles, heavy footsteps and the flash of torches.

'Holy shit. It's the police,' said Danni.

Joshua pulled her urgently, and in the darkness she had no option but to yield. She made out a fire exit, and a long concrete corridor. At the end were doors to the street. Round the corner she could hear police sirens.

'Clever of you,' she said slowly, 'to find the way out so easily.'

*　　　*　　　*

'I've been here a number of times,' he said lightly. 'I hope that didn't scare you?'

She felt bewildered more than afraid.

We've learnt *nothing*,' was all she said.

He seemed to take her words as a reproach and turned away.

'A monumental failure. I'm sorry,' he agreed. 'But at least I haven't blown your cover, such as it is. I'll drive you back to your hotel if I can just find the car.'

*　　　*　　　*

Turning round the building away from the sirens brought them to a walled restaurant and they had to retrace their steps until they found an open square. There were cars parked there, but none of them was a red Peugeot.

'I've a lousy sense of direction,' said Joshua groaning.

'Except in nightclubs,' said Rachel, thoughtfully.

*   *   *

They stopped walking and turned towards one another. Joshua was very much taller than she was. They were standing so close together that she had to tilt her chin upwards to read his face. Somewhere behind her she heard motorcycle tyres on the smooth stones, and the squeal of an excited young girl. Joshua was no longer smiling. For a moment she thought he might shake her shoulders as if she were a child. Instead, he bent his head to kiss her; a hot, open-mouthed kiss. His arms dragged her to him, so that she could feel his body against her own. He was hard and muscular as an athlete.

'Damn,' he said, when he could speak. 'Damn.'

She pulled away, bewildered by the anger in his voice.

'Will you listen to me?' he said, very seriously. 'I'll find the number you want. The telephone number of Emanuel Cellini. If I do give it to you, will you *promise* to have nothing to do with his father? Is that a deal?'

His arms still held her, but he made no move to kiss her again. After a moment's hesitation she agreed with a shrug. She was intrigued by Giorgio Cellini, but his motives

75

need not be part of her story for the *Enquirer*—Joshua seemed to have surprisingly good contacts. Perhaps too good, though she quashed that suspicion.

*   *   *

Joshua left an arm round her shoulders and they continued to walk through the streets. It was so quiet by now that she could hear the notes of her heels on the stones. They were finer heels than she usually wore, and when one caught in the cobble, she felt his arm tighten to hold her from falling.

'I'm staying in Rome because of you, Rachel O'Malley. Don't you know that?'

For a moment she thought someone had taken a hand to her lungs and pressed all the air out of them.

'What nonsense,' she said, when she could say anything.

'But I mean it. You've woken me up. I've started the first act of a new play. Now that has to be attributed to something.'

'Rome?' she suggested.

'Rome, possibly. But not only. I've decided you are my muse, Rachel O'Malley. A good, pagan muse. I hope you don't object.'

'And I thought you were such a rational man,' she murmured.

'In the *theatre*? Everyone is superstitious. Finding the same cufflinks, putting on

76

particular clothes in the same order, wearing odd socks . . .'

'Not very flattering comparisons.'

'Well, I'm not trying to flatter, I'm trying to explain. I've decided you're my talisman.'

*   *   *

She wanted to believe he meant something of what he was saying, but suspected that half of him, most of him, would always be closed away from her, and probably from everyone.

'You are such an *innocent,*' he said.

'I've knocked around more than you think,' she said indignantly.

'But you still believe people are decent. The world isn't like that. No one behaves decently any more.'

She shook her head.

'Listen,' he said. 'I've known a few women like you. Not many. Their generosity is absurd. It's outrageous, the way they let themselves be used. First they find compulsive womanisers like Christopher, then worse. They need some kind of bordello of the heart to feel ordinary excitement. Watch out, Rachel. If you discover something Cellini doesn't want known he'll have you beaten up by one of his thugs and you'll be found in an alley.'

'Surely you exaggerate?' she said uneasily. 'At lunch you said you hardly knew anything about him.'

'Don't be too clever. And that's not my only point. You don't know what a shit I am.'

'How are you a shit?'

'The usual ways. I have a bad track record. There's a woman in London I don't even like. She thinks I might marry her.'

'And will you?'

'Not a thought of it.'

'Do you have any children?'

'Yes. They are all the family I want. All I care about, really. Rachel, I am not a good bet.'

*   *   *

Even though this last exchange was absorbing most of her attention, Rachel had gradually become aware of a car rumbling through the square behind them, which now came to a halt without turning off its engine. Both of them turned when they heard a peculiar thump, as if a mail bag had been thrown out onto the street. The car, a police car, turned away and raced up a street on the opposite side of the square.

'What the hell was that?' asked Rachel breathlessly.

'It's either a body or a sack of potatoes. Stay here. I'll go and look.'

She clutched his arm.

'No. I'll come too.'

As they approached, a girl in a short white

78

dress flew across the cobbles ahead of them to where a man lay sprawled, face down, on the street.

'Ottavio, Ottavio,' she was calling in a high-pitched whine.

Joshua stopped walking.

'Probably her pimp. Shall we stay out of it?'

'But the man's hurt.'

'Yes.'

*　　*　　*

The girl brought the man to his feet, and was supporting him with one of his arms round her neck. He was a big man, much too heavy to drag, but clearly no longer insensible. He tried to take halting steps, one leg buckling as he did so.

'She could be his daughter,' suggested Rachel, reluctant to abandon the situation.

Whatever their relationship, the man had been badly beaten. His shirt was torn and covered with blood. As they approached, the girl turned her pale oval face towards them, and greeted them savagely with a stream of street Italian Rachel could not understand.

'She's telling us to piss off,' said Joshua.

'But doesn't he need a doctor?'

'I expect they'll find one.'

'Shouldn't we call the police?'

'I think the fellows who dumped him were the police. You don't clean up without a little

79

brutality. My guess is this is part of Cellini's cleaning up for the millennium.'

*   *   *

They went on walking. A clock face said three-thirty, she noticed with astonishment. As the machinery whirred and the chimes began, Joshua stopped.

'I've lost the car,' he said.

They were by now very close to the Spanish Steps and could have easily continued to her hotel but, to her surprise, he pointed to a single taxi standing alone at a rank and said, abruptly, 'It's late.'

*   *   *

Obedient, but bewildered, Rachel stepped inside the taxi, while Joshua gave the driver instructions, a handful of lire, and bent inside the car to kiss her quickly on the cheek.

'I'll be in touch,' he said.

*   *   *

And that was all. As the taxi began to move, she realised how certain she had been that they would go back to her hotel room together. She felt insulted in the most vulnerable part of herself. Only staying in Rome for her, indeed! He must have meant in

80

order to protect her from her own stupidity. Even the promise to find Emanuel's telephone number could not dull her sense of sexual rejection.

*   *   *

She began to shiver as soon as she entered the hotel foyer. It was about 4am. The usual concierge had gone off duty and the new one regarded her oddly. She could see there were no messages.

*   *   *

Even before she opened her room, she guessed what she would find. The wardrobe doors were open and a dress lay on the floor. Her books, her notes, her pencils were scattered. Someone had even opened the minibar and left the door swinging.

'I'll complain to the concierge,' she said aloud, and then remembered the odd, sly expression on his face. *He knows about it,* she decided. *He allowed it. Of course he did.*

*   *   *

The Cellini novel lay on the floor with her nightdress. She picked it up.

81

CHAPTER FOUR

It was as if time itself had been stilled. Huge silences between waking up and going downstairs, a long summer of days as bright and empty as a disused garden. How could he have endured a whole childhood of such silences? Yet they were all he could bring to mind if he tried to focus on his growing up. He had survived, as prisoners survive, by playing games. On boards. Or with the screen. Those strange selves of his own, board and screen, offered a continuity which had been broken by her departure. Alone with those selves he was not lonely. But the doctors said he must be outside, he must be playing. As if the boards did not offer exactly the kind of play he needed.

*   *   *

Apart from books. They were another solace. He read all the books that had lined her rooms; he read and lived in them. It was their perils he could remember, not his own daily life. David Copperfield's childhood was more sharply etched in his memory more packed with event and feeling, than anything else from those years. He had been educated by a black panther, or by a man who smoked opium and

82

practised a violin. All he remembered outside those enchanted pages was silence, sunshine, the garden. And chess.

*   *   *

He must have been little more than nine. In Milan. He had no memory of the chauffeur-driven car that presumably took him to that city, though he could still recall coming out through the arches of the family courtyard into the dusty village street. What he remembered was sitting in front of the grey-haired Russian with a chess clock at his right hand. There must have been many public games before that. He knew there had been; they were recorded. He had a rating. An official had pronounced him worthy to meet this famous Grandmaster.

*   *   *

He could only remember the speed of the clock, the sound of the bell as each player made their moves. And then the moment when the Russian lifted his head and offered him a draw.

*   *   *

In his memory he could still hear a hiss of astonishment rising around him as he looked down at the position before him and hesitated. He knew he was expected to accept the draw, because to have such a famous man offer it was an honour in itself. And yet he continued, staring and staring at the board patiently, as if he were alone in his room. He was more conscious of the board than the man; he could not read the line of the pieces. *Why* is he doing this? he wondered. It must be because he already knows the game is lost. He stared and stared at the board. And then, even as the Russian was already offering his hand, he saw the move.

*   *   *

He shook his head in refusal. And once again there was the hiss of astonishment, and then flashlights. Applause.

*   *   *

But all he remembered was coming home to the garden, the empty garden. There was no one in the whole of his walled life with whom he cared to share the victory. It was why, in the end, he took no great joy in it. He went out of the house into the quiet gardens, and looked at the statue of a woman holding up an urn of blessings, who might have been Calliope, the muse of poetry, and stood a long time in the moonlight until he was called for supper. He was alone except for those who looked after and spied on him.

*   *   *

Sometimes, in the kitchen, he listened to the servants grumbling to themselves at the imperious ways of their new mistress. She was a street child. A harlot. But their voices were humble enough in her presence. Even the cook was frightened to cross her. His stepmother knew about herbs and wine and how to make pastry. When she entered a room there was an electricity in her being that created a charged space around her. She put a finger in the stews and licked the juice with her thick tongue. Sometimes she shouted her orders.

*   *   *

In the evenings, when his father was away, she glittered in greens and purples. Her eyes seemed to change colour with her dress. Once he asked about that and she laughed.

—When I lived as an actress, I changed my contact lenses every night. There were twenty different shades and colours. What colour do you prefer?

—I like grey eyes, a quiet grey.

—Like your own, she teased him. You will be very handsome when you are older. But

85

now you are far too thin. Why don't you eat more?

She put another piece of beef onto his plate, ladling the aromatic juices onto his vegetables, removing a bayleaf to the side of his plate.

—I don't like to eat animals.

—Cows exist only because we eat them. Otherwise by now they would have disappeared.

—Instead they live to be butchered.

—Don't be sentimental. At least eat the sweet potatoes. Tell me. Why don't you have friends to stay? I should like to meet them. They would be very welcome.

—I don't have any friends I want to see.

—Aren't you lonely, then, living with an old woman?

She laughed and touched the black hair at the nape of her neck. Her slender throat was clasped by a coil of gold.

—No, I'm never lonely, he said.

—Do you miss your father?

—I like it when he is away.

—Do you? Then so do I. Even if we are alone in this huge house. It seems a waste, don't you think? So much space, we should have a party one night, with loud music and young people for you. Shall we arrange it?

He said nothing.

—You are hard on your father because of me.

—Not because of you.

She was impatient.

—Couldn't you try to be more affectionate? He is not unkind to you. All this is for you. This house, these paintings, this glorious cut glass. Don't you like this dinner service? I think the Romanoffs would have been pleased with it.

—The heron is very charmingly painted.

—And the painted vegetables at the edge? I particularly enjoy the artichoke. Why are you so hostile to him?

He remained silent as he pushed his food neatly to one side of his plate, and then arranged his cutlery on the other.

She sighed.

—You think it's his idea, this conversation. Of course you believe that. Well. Let me play you some American jazz. Would you like that?

—Yes, why not?

—Shall I teach you to dance? It's easy. I'll show you.

She stood up and kicked off her shoes.

—I am not so old, you see. I like to move to the music. Look. I have only to find the right record. This one. No, this one.

She rummaged carelessly in the stacks of his father's recordings.

—Today is my birthday. Birthdays are sad for me. Do you understand that?

He shook his head.

—All those books you read. What do they teach you? Listen. This is my favourite. Billie

Holiday.

When the music began, she joined her own voice to the singer's, her voice cracking over the words: 'I'm so *unhappy*.'

And suddenly her glittering eyes had the shine of tears. He stood up, not to comfort her, but to escape an emotion he did not want to understand, still less share.

Meanwhile she was staring at him.

—You should go away to school, she said. It is unnatural for you to live like this. Nothing from the real world impinges on you, you are living inside a dream. Just as I do. As if your father were dreaming us both. Shall we escape? Shall we break out together?

He did not know what to say.

She bit her underlip.

—Perhaps you are right, she said. Where could we go? After all.

He shook his head.

—Don't hate me, she pleaded.

*   *   *

School was impossible, his father explained. Too dangerous. He could not allow his child to be a hostage to fortune, to enemies of which there were only too many. Tutors, yes. That could be controlled, but not a school, away from the house.

The doctor protested. The boy must have friends. He must be allowed to run in the sunshine and fight like other boys.

—You know his condition.

—I think he could recover now, if he were in a more normal environment.

And his father had pondered.

—Tutors can come in. Boys too. The children of close friends. Very well.

But when the doctor went, he had modified his agreement.

—Piero's son. Isn't he much of an age?

*　　　*　　　*

Piero was the gardener, but perhaps not only a gardener. He was one of the men who looked after the dogs and the gardens at night, and the boy was a little afraid of him.

*　　　*　　　*

His stepmother was dubious.

—You don't understand your own son. He is very intelligent. Sensitive. The gardener's boy is a lump of clay beside him.

—I know what I am doing. It would be better for the boy if he grew up like a man, not a sensitive girl. I don't want him following his mother's path.

*　　　*　　　*

So in the daytime the boy solemnly played with

a football while the gardener's son stood in goal between two pine trees. And when they had run about for an hour or so and were pouring with sweat he would thank the boy politely and go back into the house to stand under the shower and let the hot water prickle his spine, before retreating to the cool of his own room.

*   *   *

The gardener's boy dutifully did what he was told—but when he was bored with standing in goal, he was sullen and bad-tempered and his tongue coarsened. Then the two boys would fight, which relaxed them both since they were evenly matched. One day, as they lay side by side on the grass looking up at the clouds after fighting savagely, there rose a new confidence between them, and laughter, and the gardener's boy began to talk as he ordinarily would, without caution.

—About your stepmother's arse.

—Stop it. I told you.

—What's the matter?

—I don't want to talk about stuff like that.

—I'm sorry for her. How old is she? Twenty-five? Cooped up here on her own.

—No one stops her going out.

—That's not what I heard.

—Where else would she go?

—She has a really wonderful shape. Don't

90

you think?

—I don't look at her shape. It's nothing to me, her shape.

—Well, I just wonder then. Let me look at you.

—Take your hands off my belt.

—I won't hurt you.

—Don't touch me.

—All right, all right. I'm curious, that's all. If you're old enough.

The son of the household rolled away.

—I have to go in now.

—It's hot, the other boy said. Maybe it'll rain soon. Where is your father this weekend?

—I don't know. Why?

—I heard he was away. In Palermo.

—I don't know his business.

The other boy laughed again.

—Everyone knows.

The boy of the household leant up on his arm. As he did that he looked less vulnerable, less girlishly beautiful.

—I don't think you should wonder so much. About me or my father.

—Hey now, you won't go telling anybody what we've been talking about? Will you? Where are you off to? What's so urgent suddenly?

—I solved it.

—You won't go in there and get me into any trouble now, will you?

—What kind of trouble?

—You have your tea. You just forget what I was saying.

*   *   *

The moonlight was blue on the lawn. The cypress was silver. The boy had woken in his bed to hear a dog barking, one of the guard dogs, the black ones with the ugly faces he could never trust. They were loose in the garden at night, so he wasn't allowed out then. But it wasn't the dogs that had woken him. There was a white shape in his room; a shimmering silken presence. He recognised the lit blue shadows under her cheekbones, the glitter in his eyes. It was his stepmother.

—Ssh, don't move. Don't worry. I can't sleep.

—What do you want?

—You sleep, I won't trouble you. I just want to stand here and listen. To the sound of your breath. It soothes me.

—How can I sleep with you here?

—I'll tuck in the covers.

—I don't want them on me. I like to sleep bare on a hot night.

—Throw them off then. Is that better? Sleep, I want you to sleep. I'll sit on your bed.

—There are people in the garden. I can hear them.

—Don't be frightened. If you stay awake at night you hear things. There are men to deal with everything.

—You sound frightened yourself.

—The rich are never safe. The poor are better off in the gutter.

—Why are you looking out of the window?

—Someone tried to get over the wall. It happens. Shall I lock the door?

—No, I hate that.

—I'll soothe you. Let me stroke your hair.

—I don't want you to stroke me. *You aren't my mother.* Go back to your room.

—I can't sleep alone.

—Where is my father?

—He is dealing with difficult men. Who knows if he will ever come back?

—My father always comes back.

—Perhaps you are right. He will come back as he always has.

—Where is Maria?

—I have sent her away to another part of the house.

—The dogs are going wild in the garden. Can't you hear them?

—Take no notice. Nothing is wrong. I will curl up beside you. I just want to lie at your side. I will stay and watch until you sleep. Your eyes close so easily. I envy you that. And those lashes are longer than any woman's.

CHAPTER FIVE

The Italian headlines were full of a scandal about two politicians alleged to have been involved in irregular arrangements with the tax authorities. As Rachel sat at a table reading the newspapers, the waiter hovered, ready to enter conversation.

'These politicians. They don't go to gaol. Ordinary people go to gaol, not politicians. You know my wife and I voted for Berlusconi? Different. Lots of ideas. We thought he would do very well. Now we don't even bother to vote.'

'I thought the whole world believed in democracy these days.'

'Ha? Do you know how the Americans won the cold war? Hollywood. Rita Hayworth. The Soviet government could do all the propaganda they wanted, the people wanted to live like she did. Politicians? Who cares about them?'

'What do you think of Giorgio Cellini?'

The loquacious waiter, who had been cleaning her table with a cloth quite unnecessarily in order to continue the conversation, abruptly ceased his ministrations to serve a man at the next table who wanted an ice cream. Rachel had the distinct impression that he was relieved not to answer her. She doubted he would come back and resume the discussion, but after a while he did so, though more warily.

'Cellini is a politician. What can you expect? But at least he is a man. He has my respect for that.'

'Was there ever an inquest on his first wife?' she asked. 'An autopsy?'

'Inquire into Giorgio Cellini's family?' He laughed. 'Nobody would do it.'

*　　　*　　　*

A small paragraph on the back page suddenly jumped out at her. A massive haul of cocaine in a celebrated nightclub. A singer taken away for questioning. Beside the story was the unmistakable face of the singer released on bail with charges pending. Poor Danni Alloni, she thought, a little guiltily. So much for his nice little earner.

*　　　*　　　*

She sat and thought about that. The singer's elegant gestures and silken glitter flashed before her. She could hear the American phrasing, the superbly caught Billie Holiday break in his voice. Of course Billie too had enjoyed her drugs. It wasn't *impossible* Danni would deal in them as well as use them. An elusive memory flicked into her mind but she could not hook it out.

* * *

Rachel had intended to take a short nap before Douglas Evans was supposed to collect her but sleep eluded her until about twenty minutes before he was due to arrive. She barely had time to shower, dress and rustle through her bag to find the lecture. Yet, as she pulled a comb through her hair, put a little blue shadow on her eyelids, fluffed her hair and smiled, she was not displeased with what she saw in the mirror. The lines of tiredness at her mouth and eyes had vanished in the depth of her sleep. And perhaps in her dreaming, too, she supposed, remembering a naked figure in her sleeping fantasy. Was it Giorgio Cellini, or Joshua Silk? The uncertainty made her laugh. Her imagination was not usually so dissolute. If the dream had afforded her a sexual climax, however, she had no recollection of it; all she could recall was the heaviness of a body over hers, a peculiar stillness and an imagined weight. Rome had affected her, she decided. And Emanuel's novel.

* * *

Doug was waiting for her in the green marble lobby. Twenty years after Cambridge, he remained entirely ageless: tall and bearded, without an ounce of fat on his body, still looking—with a straw hat on his head—a little like Lytton Strachey. The son of a rich family, he had never done much with his many talents, but there was no bitterness in his charm.

'Rachel, how marvellous to see you. There's a taxi rank outside so I haven't brought the Council car. Shall we go? You mustn't mind if you don't get a huge audience, by the way; Ezekiel Stern is lecturing on the canon of Eng. Lit. in another place. Sorry about that.'

'Is that where the car is?' she laughed, a little ruefully. 'You might have said there weren't going to be many people. I'd have been more relaxed writing my talk.'

'I formed the impression you had other fish to fry, anyway. How is Christopher?'

'We are *divorced*, Doug. He married again.'

'But you have someone else?'

'There's no one else,' she said. 'There was for a time, but it's over. Nothing lasts with me.'

'We'll talk afterwards,' he said.

*   *   *

The home of the British Council in Rome was at the Quattro Fontane, four fine, if grubby, sculptures at a crossroads; the offices themselves in a palace built around a courtyard. Rachel's heels clicked on shallow marble steps which were cracked and broken from the hooves of horses ridden through the building in Renaissance times. The main lecture room was set out with little more than twenty chairs, though there was room for a hundred. It had an elaborately painted ceiling, dimpled with scenes of myth and legend, with *trompe l'oeuil* stone trumpets and cherubs at the edges of every wall. Doug led her into a smaller room which boasted an ornate fireplace so valuable, he told her, that no air conditioning was allowed.

'Not allowed in the whole building, actually,' said Doug with masochistic relish. 'It gets to be like England in the worst August imaginable. But we learn to put up with it. We can open the windows onto the courtyard, of course. In the lecture room.'

Rachel could already feel perspiration running down her face; when she licked her lip it was salt.

'No wonder you don't get a large audience,' she murmured.

*   *   *

On the black wooden table Doug had set out cold wine and sweet white-fleshed cherries, and they guzzled both.

'Shouldn't we go through?' asked Rachel after a time.

Well, there's another thing,' said Doug. 'You'll have to forgive me, Rachel. There was a bit of a cock-up with the advertising. We said six-thirty in the local press and six o'clock in the handouts. So we may as well wait for the later time, don't you think?'

He poured them both another glass of wine.

'I'm in no hurry,' said Rachel. 'Tell me. What do you most enjoy about being in Rome?'

'Oh, I have a little bit of a love affair with Caravaggio,' he said. 'He is Rome for me.'

'You always did,' she remembered. 'Have you found some living human counterpart?'

It suddenly occurred to her that the homosexuality she had always taken for granted in his life might not be much indulged at the British Council.

'Like I said, we can talk afterwards.'

*   *   *

There were about thirty expatriate English at the lecture, a few more than Doug had expected. Chairs were brought from another room. Among those waiting to be seated, Rachel noticed an unexpected and formidable figure: Ingrid Donkins, who had once been her father's literary agent. It was so surprising to see Ingrid off her own central London territory that Rachel hesitated to wave and smile until the woman rose to approach her.

'*Well,* darling,' she said. 'How are *you* getting on?'

Her voice was dark, rasping from cigarettes, affectionate but challenging. One of the reasons Ingrid enjoyed a reputation for toughness was her build: she approached six foot even in flat heels, with wide shoulders, muscled arms and handsome features which looked as if they had been chiselled in stone. Her straight hair was the colour of butterscotch and fell forward in a curve at each side of her chin. Twice married, she radiated a vibrant sexuality.

'What on earth are *you* doing here?' asked Rachel, with unintentional rudeness and perhaps a touch of panic.

'I've come to give you my immoral support,' said Ingrid with a growl of a laugh. 'Aren't you pleased to see me? At least I'm an extra bum on a seat. And I might ask you the same question.'

'But I'm here to give the lecture,' said Rachel, her face dimpling. 'As you see.'

She remembered her father saying: 'Ingrid's a witch. She always knows everything. No point trying to deceive the woman.'

Ingrid clicked her teeth reprovingly at the evasion.

'I did your stars the other day, Rachel. For old time's sake.'

'You know I don't hold with all that.'

'Still, I must warn you, there were some very peculiar things in them. Very peculiar. How's Christopher, by the way?'

'Christopher,' said Rachel with a hint of frost in her voice, 'is living in Sydney on a professor's salary.'

'There you *are*,' said Ingrid delightedly. 'I *told* your father he was the one for you. Silly girl. You could be out there, lying on the sand, reading Proust, instead of hustling round the world on your own trying to earn a living. That's what comes of feminism. I told your father, but he would send you to Cambridge.'

'I had a scholarship,' Rachel pointed out, rather nettled by Ingrid's assumption that, whatever adventures she might enjoy herself, marriage remained the only option for lesser spirits.

'He couldn't afford it,' said Ingrid, as if Rachel had not spoken.

'If it comes to that, I could easily be in a home for battered wives,' Rachel pointed out.

'You English women make far too much fuss about a little masculine virility,' said Ingrid, who always spoke as if altogether detached from English life, on the grounds she was born in Cornwall and therefore a Celt. 'Christopher was just *energetic.* I liked him. Anyway you don't have to pretend. I know why you're in Rome, Rachel.'

Ingrid, who had never obeyed a 'No Smoking' notice in her life, now took out a pack of Marlboro and lit up.

'It's disgusting the way non-smokers have the rest of us completely *cowed,* as if we weren't far more likely to die from additives in food,' she said, in her usual ringing voice.

Rachel looked over towards Doug to see if he were going to take her on, but he seemed entirely occupied with urging the audience into seats.

'You're here to find the boy wonder,' said Ingrid. 'Now, aren't you?'

'Who did you hear that from?' demanded Rachel.

'Oh, the world of expat English here is very small. Diplomats, journalists and so forth. I can't remember who told me. I do think you should leave all that alone, Rachel. You're a sweet child with a head full of Latin poetry. Which is how it should be. You don't want some foolish Roman gangster to think you live by putting your pretty little nose into other people's sewers, do you? Your father wouldn't have approved.'

'What do you know about Roman gangsters?' asked Rachel.

'My dear! *Have* you read the boy's book? Never would have guessed the child had it in him.'

Rachel felt a ripple of pleasurable interest.

'You've met the boy himself?' she asked hopefully.

'Long ago,' said Ingrid. 'I knew the mother. Not the mad one who jumped over the balcony—I'm sure she was a complete drag. I mean the second wife. Now she was a remarkable woman.'

'In what way?' asked Rachel, her eyes alight.

'Well, stunning looks, for a start. She gave the most marvellous parties in Rome.'

'And where is she now?'

* * *

At precisely this moment, and before Ingrid could answer, Doug came over to say it was a little past six-thirty and the lecture really ought to begin, so Rachel had to follow him meekly to the dais with her question unanswered. A thousand questions rattled in her mind. But we can talk *afterwards,* she thought, as Doug gave his amusing, improvised introduction.

* * *

Rachel began by expounding the paradox of the disparity between Seneca's own sybaritic life and the austere Stoicism of his moral writings.

'You'll know,' she continued, 'there's rather a similar gap between the Seneca who wrote moral essays and the writer of poetic tragedies based on Greek models. Scholars seem to be agreed that both were written by the same hand yet, as a moral teacher, Seneca urged people to curb their passions while in his melodramas every opportunity is taken both to indulge the passions and to express them.'

103

As a woman, Rachel continued, she was particularly interested in Phaedra and the way Seneca's treatment of her differed from that of Euripides, and she developed that theme for the rest of the talk.

*   *   *

For all the heat, the audience listened well enough. Most of them were women, mainly English, though one or two young men looked Italian. Afterwards, the questions were desultory and had little to do with the lecture. There were questions about Seneca's corrupt financial dealings, and the cowardice in his failed suicide, which she couldn't answer. They went on long enough, however, for Ingrid to rise and walk in great, confident strides from the room. Rachel stared after her. Whatever Ingrid had wanted to learn from the evening she must have already discovered, or else decided there was nothing more to be gained. The rudeness of the departure was mitigated by her pause at the door to smile and wave. She might have come to warn Rachel off, but she was evidently well-disposed.

*   *   *

'Do you *know* Ingrid?' Rachel demanded, when the audience had dispersed.

'I know who she is, of course,' said Doug.

'Her sister was at school with mine, now I think of it.'

'My father always said she got him launched. But she must be the rudest woman alive.'

'Sent her my novel once, but she sent it straight back,' muttered Doug. 'Well, I suppose she was right. What is she doing in Rome?'

'I don't know,' said Rachel.

*   *   *

Doug took her to eat at Pierluigi's near the Campo de' Fiori, at a table set out under an awning. Against the dark blue of the sky, the illuminated wall opposite glowed a Van Gogh yellow. Doug ordered crab salad, fried balls of courgette flowers and olives. Other dishes followed as they talked.

'It's too much,' she protested.

'Everything in Rome is too much. Now tell me. *What* are you up to? Did you really come here to give a talk about Senecan tragedy and enjoy a bit of tourism?'

She hesitated. Doug was a great gossip.

'The idea was to earn a few grand. Which I much need. If I could get to Emanuel Cellini, I've got an English Sunday ready to print what I write. Can you help at all?'

'Depends what kind of help you need.'

'I mean, have you *seen* him, do you know

105

anything about him?'

'Awkward as it is, I must confess I do.'

Rachel caught her breath.

'How do you?'

'He's very beautiful. Or he was. Rachel, I don't want to be disingenuous, but I don't want to end up in your English Sunday either. I fell in love with him. Long before his book came out.'

'Where did you meet him?'

'A gay bar,' said Doug. 'But do keep that under your hat. Or at least out of your article.'

'So he's gay, then?'

'I don't think so. Or, if he is, he doesn't know it. I don't think he's *anything* sexual. But, naturally, a few of us liked the look of him. At a distance, however.'

'Why was he in the bar, then?' she asked.

'I think he just drifted in off the street. Maybe he lived nearby.'

'Someone must know him.'

Well, he never talked to anyone.'

'Did he go there more than once?'

'A few times. No one tried to pick him up, though, once the barman whispered who he was,' said Doug. 'We just eyed him. Lasciviously.'

'I don't know much about these places, but isn't that unusual?'

'Well, Cellini is an unusual figure.'

'I bet someone took the risk. Which bar is it?'

'It's been shut down,' said Doug, 'because, ironically enough, Cellini *père* is cleaning up the city for the millennium.'

'I thought he used to be head of the underworld?'

'Who better to clean it up?' asked Doug.

*   *   *

A burst of laughter distracted Rachel's attention towards a group at the far end of the awning. There she recognised Joshua Silk, elegantly poised with one foot on a chair, his gestures unembarrassed, his flow of anecdote, to judge by the response of his audience, exquisitely comic. If he had seen Rachel, he gave no sign of it.

'Ah yes,' said Doug, following her gaze. 'I heard he was still in Rome.'

As Joshua talked, Rachel watched one delicate hand position the blonde head of the girl at his side, as if to illustrate a point. The girl submitted with a pleased smile. Perhaps he was commenting on her performance that evening. But Rachel observed that his hand remained gently on her slender neck as he continued to speak.

'An actress,' said Doug. 'Pretty, if you like that kind of kitten face.'

'I suppose *she* is the reason he is still here,' said Rachel, her voice a little hollower than before.

Doug shrugged.

'Is he still married?' Rachel asked, as casually as she could.

'No idea. He mentioned three small children in a newspaper interview. If he is, they'll have one of those modern marriages, wouldn't you think? Both of them doing as they like. And a lot to be said for it. Kinder to children than serial monogamy. No wicked stepfathers. Did your parents divorce, by the way?'

*　　*　　*

Doug was pouring the rest of the wine into his own glass as he spoke, and was waving at the waiter for another bottle. Rachel had stopped listening to him, though she was conscious of a lengthy confession. The niggling thought that had been disturbing her since reading the newspaper paragraph about the singer had just flicked up into her mind. She remembered very clearly the odour of cachou breath as Alloni bent over them. A warning *before* the police arrived? Not an ordinary drugs bust, then.

*　　*　　*

'Never saw my own father again,' Doug continued, unabashed by her failure to respond. 'Just a ghost I could puzzle over in photographs. I couldn't have managed without my mother. She was, and still is, the linchpin of my life.'

'*Is?*' exclaimed Rachel. '*Where* is she?'

'She lives here in Rome, of course.'

'With you?'

'Where else?'

At that moment Rachel's eyes met Joshua's and, to her irritation, she could feel her colour rising. He made her a mischievous bow.

'We could join them if you like,' suggested Doug, who might be rather drunk and obsessional but was not stupid. 'It looks quite informal.'

Whatever for?' asked Rachel crossly.

*   *   *

Doug returned to his own narrative and, in the event, it was Joshua who came over to them.

'You didn't call,' he said pleasantly to Rachel, 'so I imagine your Roman pursuit goes well. Good evening, Doug. Let me buy you both one of those wonderful Italian liqueurs they drop coffee beans into.'

'Sambucca is too sweet for me,' said Rachel.

Joshua accepted her ungraciousness with an imitation of a downcast schoolboy and said, in a mock Irish brogue, exaggerated, she supposed, in her honour, 'That's an unkind response, Miss O'Malley, so it is. When all I'm wanting is to pay respects to you, as Zuleika

Dobson of the fens.'

'I should think another glass of the red would serve for that,' said Doug. 'And I wouldn't refuse.'

'Not for me,' said Rachel, rather nastily.

And then Joshua grinned, a deep grin which scored lines across his cheekbones, as if he suddenly understood why Rachel was behaving so badly. He sat down astraddle a chair, looking, she thought, like a tall and possibly dangerous dog deciding on obedience. Against her will, she could feel her mouth widen to a relenting smile. As Joshua saw as much, their eyes met. For a moment, her desire returned so powerfully that her head swam.

*   *   *

'We were talking about *families,*' said Doug, perfectly aware of that flash of sexual electricity but disinclined to move off into his own world.

'Had no childhood myself. I was born fully formed as an adult, as far as I remember,' said Joshua. 'No complaints. Wonderful luxury, childhood, but quite possibly boring in large doses.'

*   *   *

Unforgivably, Rachel wanted Doug to leave at once, with an impatience she had last

110

experienced in a queue for a photocopier. Instead of going, however, Doug called for more wine, and went on about his stepfather's coldness and his mother's stalwart spirit, until at last he got to his feet unsteadily to say, 'I'll cry if I stay any longer. Don't often have the chance to talk. Don't worry about paying or anything, will you?'

*   *   *

His departure left a great silence in its wake. Rachel felt completely exposed to Joshua's presence. The single candle at the table seemed to hold the two of them together as if they were floating alone in a circle of its light, with the rest of the café lost in darkness.

'I've been a bit presumptuous. Sorry,' said Joshua. 'I hope it's all right, barging in like this? I mean Doug. Everyone knows about Doug.'

'I never knew how *sad* he was,' said Rachel.

'It's not a particularly savage history, if you were listening,' said Joshua. 'Though I suppose it is always surprising how certain patterns repeat themselves again and again. Not in my case, however. No parents. No memories.'

'Why not? What's all this about being born old?'

'A child can't remember anything that happens before he's two. Well, that's roughly when I was brought to England.'

111

'1956?' she calculated slowly.

'That's it. Better dead than Red, Russian tanks in Budapest, radio calls for help. That's how they show it on the telly documentaries. Funny to think about, now there are Western chain stores in Vaci Street.'

'And your mother and father?'

'My aunt and uncle brought me up,' he said. 'I'm living proof of the power of nurture. But to get back to the case in hand, I've been working hard on that telephone number. Now, Cellini and I share a publisher. According to him, Cellini's royalties go to charity. He's never had an agent; the manuscript just arrived in the slush pile. No mail is to be forwarded to him, so there's no address. It's almost as if the boy doesn't exist.'

'How do we know he *does* exist? Apart from the book?'

'Well, he has a birth certificate. I've checked that. And there's no sign of him dying. Of course, he *could* be living in Switzerland, which would not be a bad bet with his father as an enemy.'

'The dustjacket says he lives in Rome.'

'That would hardly be the first lie so promulgated.'

'I hadn't thought of that,' she said, crestfallen.

'However, such is not the situation,' said Joshua.

'You've found something out?'

'You do remember the promise?'

'Of course,' she said impatiently. 'But how have you managed it? And why aren't you scared, if you're so frightened for me?'

'I actually *enjoy* a permanent adrenaline rush of terror. Let me tell you the story. I became aware that my line of questioning was leading my publisher to perspire even though the air in his office was chilled to New York temperatures. It suddenly occurred to me that he might not be telling me the whole truth. Why the hell should he, after all? It was hardly his habit. So . . . I asked to see my royalty statements.'

'That doesn't sound like much of a threat.'

'Nor is it. But, as I hoped, he buzzed his secretary to get them, and then he had someone else to see while she was looking them out. So I was able to hang around his office while he nipped along the corridor . . . It was in his computer, Rachel. I found it using *Sherlock*. So. That's Cellini's number,' he said, bringing out a card. 'Until the end of next week.'

That's absolutely *wonderful.*'

He looked at her quizzically.

'You aren't afraid to use it?'

She thought of the ruffled clothes, the books and papers on the floor of her room. But all she felt was excitement.

'I don't feel the *boy* is dangerous,' she said. 'Do you? Neurotic, perhaps, but not mad.'

'You wouldn't like me to come with you, just in case?'

'It wouldn't work, would it? He just *might* see me, but he'd feel threatened if there were two of us.'

'The English always like to play tough when there's danger. Lack of imagination, probably.'

*   *   *

Rachel suddenly remembered Danni Alloni.

'Did you notice in the newspaper . . .' she began, but he was ahead of her.

'I tried to visit Danni this morning. But he's gone to ground.'

'Maybe he's trying to raise the bail.'

'No. He'd already been warned off seeing me. Naturally, he wasn't about to see me today either. Tell me your plan,' he said.

*   *   *

When she returned to the hotel, there was a little flurry of excitement behind the receptionist's desk, where the grim-faced man usually offered no more than a curt shake of the head.

'Signora, signora, you have messages.'

His hitherto expressionless face had broken open into excitement. And indeed there were two messages. The first was a laconic fax from Indonesia which said:

'Bali is amazingly beautiful, but I'm off to Sumatra now, which I am promised is pretty much in the Stone Age. Don't worry. Love, Tom.'

Just to see the newly familiar Palatino typeface of his laptop sent a flood of relief coursing through every vein in Rachel's body. But it was the second, the enormous cellophane-wrapped bouquet of flowers that had brought such joy to the man behind the desk. Its splendour was indeed bewildering: roses of a fresh honey-yellow mingled with tall tiger lilies and delicate pale green ferns. The receptionist could hardly disguise his curiosity as Rachel searched for the envelope to find who could have sent her such a magnificent bouquet.

'A chauffeur in a white car,' he volunteered. 'He brought it not twenty minutes ago. Shall I have them put in a vase and taken up to your room?'

'Yes, do,' she said, automatically.

The attached note from Giorgio Cellini invited her to dinner two days later. It was not exactly couched as an invitation: a car would collect her from the hotel at six o'clock, he suggested; would she telephone his secretary if the arrangement inconvenienced her? Rachel was flattered and puzzled, and in no way disposed to refuse. She had not forgotten her promise to Joshua, but she felt wickedly unwilling to be bound by it. What she did not ask herself, as the mirrored lift rose smoothly to her fifth floor, was exactly *why* she wanted to see Giorgio Cellini now she had a way of contacting his son. He was possibly dangerous, and surely unsuitable; but then Joshua had suggested much the same of himself.

*   *   *

Once in her room, Rachel paced around uncertainly, waiting for someone to bring up the vase of flowers, and thinking hard. Even after the flowers had arrived and been set on the table in all their splendour, she found it impossible to settle. She would have to sleep before she tried to ring the telephone number she had been given, yet she felt hopelessly awake. She would look again at the novel, she determined, and ring first thing in the morning.

CHAPTER SIX

A child lay in her belly, she said. She thought it might be him, at first, then she thought it might be his child and puzzled at that. How could a child of his find its way inside her? In the dream there was no explanation. He wasn't even sure whether he had remembered the dream correctly.

116

*   *   *

It was too hot that July. An African heat. On the birch trees, the leaves were already brown, the house beginning to creak and shift. Builders arrived with talk of subsidence and underpinning. Then clouds gathered. The town lights coloured the wetness in the sky. All the decisions were to be left for his father's return.

*   *   *

Then there was a rainy night in high summer. The gardens smelled of rain, even though there was a July heat in the stones. That day he had spent alone in the garden, studying hard, until his head hurt from the heat and the pages went blurry under his eyes. There were lime tree seeds in his hair, and his scalp was too sensitive for him to comb them out. In the cool of the servants' lavatory he had been sick. Heat stroke, Maria said, sending him early to bed. When he woke it was still the middle of the night. He found it luxurious just to lie drowsing, not asleep, enjoying the huge yellow moon, almost full, that had taken up its summer station in the branches of the tree outside his window. The window was open. In his fantasy, he imagined himself rolling in its light, tasting the night air, washing himself in

117

the warm rain, and so ridding himself of the ache in his temples, but it was too late to walk in the gardens because of the dogs.

*   *   *

She often came to his room. Sometimes he did not even waken. Sometimes she simply sat at his side. Sometimes they talked.

*   *   *

—It's your birthday tomorrow. What will you do?

—I shall work on Virgil.

—You could take the day off.

—The exams are too close.

—Your report gave you an 'A' in everything. You don't need to work so hard.

—It's what I like.

—What will you do when you grow up?

—I haven't planned.

—Do you never feel you need someone to love you?

—I don't know what that means.

—But you remember your mother?

—A little.

—What do you remember?

—She was soft and gentle and my father made her cry.

—If she was gentle, then you must have loved her.

—I was sorry for her.

—Let me sit on your bed.

—If you like.

—Shall I comfort you? Take your hand, as a mother would.

—If you want to.

—I am so lonely. You can't imagine how desperately lonely.

—When you talk of love . . .

—Yes . . .

—Do you love my father?

—Once I loved him, yes. I told him: whatever you want me to do I shall do, go or stay, at your will. And he said stay. So here I am.

—But now?

—Now I'm a caged animal. Help me.

—How can I help you?

—Love me. I have no child of my own.

—I've told you. I don't know what the word means.

—You can't be so cold. Your face is so tender.

—There is an English fairy tale. I think it is English. My mother read it to me.

—I don't read English.

—About a splinter of ice in the heart.

—It is a fairy tale.

—Why do you look at me so intensely? You are trembling.

—I have not been well.

—Are you cold?

—No. I have a fever.

—You should call someone to look after you.

—I only need an iced drink.

—There is some lemon water on the little chest. There. But it is not very cold.

—Thank you.

—Your hand is shaking. You are dropping water on the sheet.

—It doesn't matter. I want to talk to you. Your hair is fair as a child of the North. Once all the richest men in Rome wanted me. When I was young.

—People still look at you.

—Who looks? Who dares to look? Listen to me. Have you ever seen a girl you wanted to touch?

—Once I saw what men do with girls.

—Where did you see such a thing?

—The gardener's boy. He showed me photographs.

—Your father should explain these things to you.

—I am *glad* he is away from home.

—Are you? Do you know what I'm feeling?

—I don't know what anyone is feeling.

—Put your hand on my breast. Now. Tell me what you feel.

—Your heart is banging. It is going too fast, much faster than mine.

—And what else?

—You are shivering.

—Can you feel nothing else?

—I can feel your body under the silk.

—Dear God.

—Shall I leave my hand where it is?

—Bring it lower. Are you frightened?

—Is this what you want me to do?

—Here. Yes. And here. Dear God.

—And here?

—I am not a wicked woman.

—But I want to do what you like.

—Yes, then yes. But you must say nothing, you will tell no one, not a friend, not a servant, no one, my life is in your hands.

—No one.

—If you do, I shall lie. I have experience in lying. No one will believe you. They will think this is something you have invented. They say you are strange. Did you know that? No one will believe you. No one. Do you understand?

—There is no one I could tell.

—Let me touch your body. Dear God, how strong you are . . . You are very young.

*   *   *

And July continued. He talked to no one about those moments in the night when she came to him. But then, whom did he see that he could tell? When she did not come for a few days he was anxious, and left his own room to see where she was. And she explained to him gravely how blood came from her body

121

every month, that she did not want to frighten him. She took him in her arms nevertheless, and he fell asleep in her bed.

*   *   *

And then in early September, in the first shock of cold rain, with the wind shaking the leaves in the garden, he heard angry voices.

*   *   *

He was in his own room. His limbs were ungainly, uncomfortable; his skin wet. He was dreaming. Of someone struggling in a tree, her hair caught up in the branches. Someone swinging like a tassel. He woke with his heart pounding. Impossible to sleep in the sullen heat. Then, just before morning, the rain began. Heavy rain. He must have fallen asleep because he woke listening to it. Through open windows the pink tiles were shining in grey light. Then he heard angry voices. Running feet.

—You street slut.
—Why do you believe Maria?
—I'll kill you if you don't tell me.
—There's nothing to confess.
—Keep still. I know Maria. I pay her.
—Take your hands off my throat.
—Who was he?
—There is no one.

—She washes your sheets. She knows.

—You are hurting me.

—Talk then.

—Maria is a liar.

—Whose semen did she find in my bed?

—If you slap me again I'll tell you nothing.

—You'll tell me. Now. Tell me.

—My mouth is bleeding.

—Tell me.

—Only if you listen.

—I know how to listen.

—Then put your hands down. All right. I didn't know where you were.

—Go on.

—Don't you know the kind of woman I am? Isn't that why you wanted me?

—Bitch.

—So what do you expect? You were away. I was frightened.

—You don't know what it is to be afraid. You admit it then?

—Let me breathe.

—Who? Some houseboy? Gardener? Tell me and I'll take off his balls with my own knife.

—What makes you think there was only one?

—You whore.

—You knew that when you married me. Look. Over there.

*   *   *

123

The boy was standing in the doorway to the library. He saw his stepmother had a trickle of blood on her chin; a streak of it ran down her golden neck into the perfect curve of her breast where her dress was torn.

—Go back to bed, said his father impatiently, without looking at him.

But the boy did not move.

The woman straightened her dress, caught sight of her own reflection, made a little comic expression and took out her compact, dabbing at her lips, and wiping away the blood from her neck.

*   *   *

What are you doing on this side of the house? his father growled. Go back to your room.

She clicked her compact shut and moved to stand between them. He could see the blood still running where her lip had caught in her teeth; there was a bruise already swelling under one of her eyes.

—I heard shouts. What is happening?

—Nothing. What should be the matter?

—There are bruises on her shoulder.

—Grown-up games. Nothing. Go back to sleep.

—Don't be angry with her.

—I'll call Maria. She can take you back to bed.

124

—No. First take your hands off her.

—I'll give you a beating you won't forget if you keep on standing there!

—For God's sake, would you hit your own child? Are you mad? I'm not worth it.

—No. You aren't. Go and pack.

*   *   *

Through the window came rain smells. Blown rose and jasmine. His bed was at the level of the beech trees. He could see the wind moving the branches. The sound of the rain on the grass. It filled his room. When she came to say goodbye, she was dressed in a loose green dress and carried a raincoat.

*   *   *

—I came to thank you.

—I did nothing.

—You were very brave.

—I couldn't help you. Now I see why you say I'm too thin.

—How sweetly you smile. And sadly. It was your smile I loved first. But of course you are far too thin. It's because you don't eat as you should. And you should cut your hair, it takes the strength out of your body. Did you have your eyes checked like you promised?

—There's nothing wrong with my eyes. Don't pretend. I know what's going to happen.

—I want to warn you. Listen. Don't get too close to Maria.

—Why would I? She's so stupid.

—But sly. She's crafty. Don't trust her.

—Why would I get close to her?

—I don't know. You were always shy. But she's still a young woman. When I go, will you be sorry?

—Must you go?

—You don't blame me, then?

—He is so strong, did he make you? Did he make you do that?

—Listen. You mustn't hate your father.

—Did he make you do what he wanted?

—Don't think about him.

—It's my father sends you away, isn't it?

—I would have to go. What else could happen?

—He wants to punish me.

—Silly child. It is me he is punishing.

—Your face is white, and your dress is wet.

—Listen, be quiet and listen. If he tries to ask you, tell him nothing.

—Why should I talk to him? I never talk to him. He doesn't care.

—Listen. Please. Don't make your father angry.

—I don't care about his anger.

—Have you seen the way he looks at you? Even before this. As if he cursed you in his heart.

—I don't care about his curse.

—A father's curse is very powerful.

—I don't think so.

—Yes. It enters the soul. It lives in the soul.

—I don't believe in the soul.

—What nonsense. Everyone has a soul. Everything that wants to live.

—You mean like that birch tree?

—Well, and trees too. They want to live. Why else would they push out of the earth, and fight for air and sky?

—Everything fights.

—No, everything wants to live.

—You think so?

—Listen. When you stop wanting to live, you're like an old man in a chair with that disease—the name I forget . . .

—You mean Alzheimers'.

—That's it, such a clever boy you are.

—Listen. I'm not important.

—He *did* hit you, didn't he?

—He was right to hit me. —What did you tell him?

—I told him nothing. Forget about me.

—Why do you ask me to forget?

—Your father wants to be loved. He's lonely too. He's had a hard life.

—Why should I love him if he wants something bad to happen to me?

—Love someone. Something. Forget about me.

—When are you leaving?

—Tomorrow, early.

—Why is your face wet?

—It's good you feel something for me.

—Are you crying?

—I'm afraid for you.

—Because of my father? I don't care about him.

—He is clever and dangerous.

—I know. He won't make me *care*, though.

—He will do something.

—Will you come back and see me?

—I don't think so.

*　　　*　　　*

All the darkness of time. Books and time. And only the seasons changing. A bitterly cold winter. A late spring. Another year and then, at eighteen, his inheritance. In September he could live in Rome. Until then, he preferred to stay in his room. He felt happiness only when he was alone, with the curve of the road rising under his new car, on his computer screen. A solitary joy. He knew it was as dangerous as any other addiction. People went mad in it. Perhaps he had. It was hard to remember. But there was always Maria to chivvy him.

*　　　*　　　*

—Come down for supper. Your father sent me to get you.

—Tell him I want to eat in my room. I'm

working. You can see I'm working.

—You can't sit here in the dark.

—There's a desk light.

—What are you doing that's so important?

—You can see.

—Leave it. Come down. He is angry.

—I don't care about that.

*   *   *

—You spend too long in front of that screen, his father said. I'll have it taken away.

—Why would you do that?

—It's not healthy.

—I learn from it.

—You'll turn into a mess of digital bleeps. Maybe you already have. Learn what, anyway? More games? Do you play chess up there, is that it? You think too much of that brain of yours. Who gave you such a high opinion of yourself?

—No one.

—You think you will ever amount to anything?

—I don't know.

—I can tell you. You won't.

—Then it doesn't matter.

—You'll never be a man. Look at you. I could break you like a twig.

—Why does it worry you, what I do?

—You should get some exercise. Develop your muscles. Suppose I wanted to leave my

129

affairs in your hands?

—I don't want to take over your affairs.

—What kind of life will you have?

—I shall live in a flat in Rome when I go to the university.

—Only if I agree.

—I have money of my own.

—But I am still your father.

—Yes.

—You are nothing, do you hear me? Nobody.

—I know that.

—Very well. Eat your supper.

CHAPTER SEVEN

Rachel rang the number she had been given for Emanuel Cellini immediately after her morning coffee. She had thought out exactly what to say. She would explain she was an academic, not a journalist; a writer on Roman poets; she was particularly interested in modern retellings of classical legends; she had loved his novel; perhaps he would see her and tell what had drawn him to the story of Phaedra.

*   *   *

The telephone was answered almost

immediately.

'Pronto,' said a young male voice.

Could this be the reclusive genius?

'My name is Rachel O'Malley,' she began. 'Your number was given to me last night. I hope you don't mind my calling.'

'A friend I respect told me about you. I'm glad you called.'

And then she did experience a moment of fear. She had told no one. Who could know? Who had alerted him? She frowned. She did not want to begin distrusting Joshua.

'I know your name,' he explained. 'My mother would have wanted me to see you.'

'I'm in Rome another three days. When could we meet?'

'Maybe tomorrow.'

'For lunch?'

'Yes, lunch. About 1pm. But I don't like to go out to eat. Will you be able to find my apartment?'

'If you give me your address, I shouldn't think there'll be a problem.'

She bit back another thought—her delight in the chance to see his apartment—fearing it might sound only too evidently that of a journalist. When she put down the phone, she capered round the room in triumph.

*   *   *

For a moment she paused in her dance. Why,

then, was she going to have dinner with this Giorgio Cellini? No reason, now she had arranged to see Emanuel. He had left it perfectly easy for her to refuse. She might, after all, have another appointment; he could hardly object to that. But she knew she was not going to do any such thing, that she *wanted* to have dinner with him. Even if he had warned Joshua's friend off talking to her. Even if he had some illicit connection to the Mafia. He had made his sexual interest evident. And she was not averse to his attentions. On the contrary, she was deeply flattered. And in that flattery she felt a darker response. She knew she was taking a risk, and the thought made her feel more alert and alive.

*   *   *

She was certainly jeopardising her relationship with Joshua, but even as Rachel let Joshua's warning words return to her memory, and conjectured about the source of her own feelings, the telephone rang at her bedside. The voice she recognised instantly was that of Ingrid Donkins.

'*Darling!*' she said. 'I'm sorry I rushed off so rudely but there you were, mobbed by your admirers, and I had to meet a friend for a drink. What about lunch today?'

'I thought I would do a little sightseeing,' said Rachel, evasively. The last thing she wanted at this emotional juncture was to submit herself to Ingrid's close examination.

'Well, but you have to eat *somewhere,* don't you?' said Ingrid reasonably. 'You can sightsee first. *This* is on me. I know a marvellous place. Your father always trusted my taste in restaurants.'

*   *   *

As she soaped herself moodily under the shower, Rachel wondered why Ingrid was being so friendly. As a child, she had always found her alarming, even though in those days Ingrid was in her twenties, just starting out. All she had then was her uncanny certainty of guessing *right.* So what was she guessing now? Rachel had no intention of divulging Emanuel's telephone number, if that was what Ingrid was after. Or confiding her own arrangements. As she dried herself with a deep green towel, however, she had a crafty thought of her own: Ingrid might be able to tell her something about both wives of Signor Cellini. Rachel's interest by now was not only focused on the article she was trying to write: she needed to learn as much as she could about Giorgio himself.

*   *   *

'I will see one or two beautiful objects only,'

133

thought Rachel, remembering her last visit to the Forum, where she had spent a sweaty hour or two, and lost the heel of her shoe, in pursuit of the newly excavated house of Augustus' Empress Livia. She decided to make for the Capitoline museums, since their frescoed walls were beautiful in themselves, and Doug had reminded her there was a particularly beautiful Caravaggio she had never seen.

*　　*　　*

She found the painting he meant without much difficulty and sat down to look at it: a painting of St John the Baptist. The figure of the saint glowed against the darkness of the rest of the picture space; his body was sensuously naked, and there was a ram nuzzling his face. While hardly the usual image of the austere forerunner of Christ, the figure was painted with less aggression than those in other Caravaggios she knew, and she could see why Doug loved it. The face of the young man was laughing and open, and he turned over his shoulder to greet the spectator, even as he embraced his animal friend. The paint conjured the feel of young flesh; the same delicate pink had been used for loins, tender heels and the unexcited, uncircumcised penis.

*　　*　　*

An Italian in a rather shabby suit sat down at a little distance to watch the same painting. Or perhaps to watch *her*? He seemed to give little attention to the painting. She decided Joshua Silk was making her paranoid. Why shouldn't the man just sit and rest his legs, if it came to that.

*   *   *

She gave herself a quiet hour in front of the painting, and then planned a quick tour of the rest of the museum before crossing the square designed by Michelangelo to look for a taxi. She spent longer looking at Marcus Aurelius' horse than she'd intended. The Roman sun stood at its height; it was just after midday. The Italian who had been sitting on the bench near the Caravaggio stood in the queue behind her as a taxi arrived to take her away. She watched idly as he pulled out a mobile phone and began to gesticulate as he talked into it. She was amused at the animation of his whole body as he spoke, as if he could not talk without moving his hands.

*   *   *

The restaurant Ingrid had chosen was furnished with stark modernity: armchairs and sofas in glass, tubular steel and leather, the hand of Le Corbusier or Cassina everywhere.

135

'You look a bit overheated,' said Ingrid. She was looking, in contrast to Rachel, beautifully cool. 'Do you like my outfit? I bought it in London. Ghost.'

'Ghost?'

'Darling, you *must* have heard of Ghost. They make the most marvellous clothes. What were you thinking of—something spooky?' Ingrid gave her throatiest laugh. 'Let's order, then we can talk.'

'I think I'd better wash first,' said Rachel. 'All these people here look as if they'd just stepped out of *Elle*.'

'I'll get you something iced for when you're back.'

'I'll have a Punt a Mes,' said Rachel.

'With ice and lemon? I hate it myself. Better in Italy, I suppose. In London it always tastes like medicine,' said Ingrid, with that enormous authoritative slowness she put into her most casual pronouncements.

*   *   *

Rachel retreated to the brilliantly lit room, washed her face, combed her hair and was not pleased with what she could see in the mirror. Her colour was too high. Sightseeing that morning had been a mistake, she reflected; a legacy of her father's obstinacy, which he always described as determination.

136

* * *

Emerging with as cool a gaze as she could manage, Rachel found Ingrid deep in consultation with the waiter.

'I have ordered,' Ingrid announced. 'Trust me. It will be magnificent.'

'I'm *sure*,' said Rachel, too hot in any case to be hungry. 'Why did you want to see me, I couldn't help wondering?'

'I promised Frank I'd look after you if you ever showed the slightest signs of wanting to write for a living, which is not a mistake I expected you to make. Now I'm worried. How *can* you work for the *Sunday Enquirer*?'

'Much-needed money,' said Rachel promptly.

'Well, in that case, let me distract you with some good news, and perhaps you'll reconsider. Your father's novels are having a revival. The Italians are reissuing them this year. Indeed, that is why I am here. They say he will remind people of the grandeur of Ancient Rome—'

'Ancient corruption, more like,' said Rachel. 'Anyway, I wouldn't have thought translation rights would bring in much.'

'Don't be clever. The Americans are next. And that will make a very substantial difference to you. Rachel, all this skidding around looking for dirty secrets doesn't suit you. I'll think of something better, something

137

you can respect yourself for.'

Rachel was astonished.

'Why would you bother?'

'I always go on my hunches,' said Ingrid. You're a late starter, but something has changed in you, I can see that. It's a question of getting your energy to connect with the right project. And your translations were promising.'

'My only book disappeared without so much as a review,' said Rachel.

'One review,' Ingrid corrected.

'Yes, but so unfavourable I hoped no one would read it,' said Rachel, not at first registering the surprising wealth of Ingrid's information. 'In any case, I thought you disapproved of writing women.'

'Most of them. But you *are* Frank's daughter. And you don't whinge. How's your piece going, by the way?'

'Nothing new yet,' said Rachel, with her bluest, most open-eyed smile.

*   *   *

Over Ingrid's shoulder she made out two men entering the restaurant who were at first refused a table, since the restaurant was full. The manager must have known them, however, because he made a place for them at a side table. They did not look particularly important, Rachel thought idly. Indeed their

138

suits were older than those of the other clientèle and decidedly less well-cut; their faces blank and bored. Was one of them the man who had shared her bench at the Capitoline museum?

*   *   *

She took a deep drink of wine. As his face turned, she was suddenly sure of it. So, she *was* being followed.

'By the way, I advise you not to have too much to do with Joshua Silk,' said Ingrid.

'Why?'

The two men had begun to order a meal. Rachel wondered if she should explain the situation to Ingrid and simply slip away.

'Joshua makes trouble for the fun of it,' said Ingrid flatly. 'And he's a liar.'

Rachel considered that.

'How well do you know him?'

'Everyone knows him. Anyway, give up all this Cellini nonsense.'

Rachel bit her lip. No one seemed to think she could look after herself.

'Look, I could give you an *advance* on Frank's money if you like.'

'Very generous. I won't refuse. But I can't promise to go home, just because you say so.'

'You are a very stubborn girl,' said Ingrid, with a splendid, indulgent laugh.

For a moment the two men who were sitting

139

very still at the table near the door looked up, startled. Had Cellini put them there and, if so, what did he hope they would prevent? Rachel wondered. She now had no intention of saying anything about them to Ingrid.

There had to be another way out of the restaurant, but while she looked for it, by far the best decoy she could have was Ingrid left behind solemnly waiting for her return. And, in any case, she had an agenda of her own, a question she wanted to ask before leaving. So she went along cheerfully enough with Ingrid's good humour, accepting another glass of wine.

'Will you have a sweet?' asked Ingrid.

'I don't think so,' said Rachel.

'Your father never refused *anything* in Cointreau,' said Ingrid dreamily, and for a second Rachel was diverted into wondering what kind of relationship Ingrid had shared with him. 'I was a bit disappointed you didn't mention his novel, by the way,' Ingrid went on. 'You do remember, don't you, that he wrote a novel about Seneca?'

'Of course.'

'Well, that's the one they're going to bring out first. I always thought it was his best. I think that would have pleased him. I suppose you academics have no time for the intuitive reading of history?'

'I'm far from an academic, alas,' said Rachel. 'Missed my chance there.'

'He had a very fine imagination, your

140

father,' said Ingrid. 'I *hoped* you'd give it a plug.'

'It never occurred to me,' said Rachel. 'But I haven't forgotten Dad was the first one to interest me in Horace and Catullus.'

'I'm glad you appreciated him,' said Ingrid. 'So many children these days have no time for their relations. Do you see your mother?'

'Not often,' said Rachel. 'We don't really get on.'

*   *   *

Then she asked, casually: 'You did mention you knew the second Signora Cellini. I've heard a few stories about her from Joshua. What was she like?'

'Really, Rachel, I thought you'd have more sense than to listen to his kind of gossip,' said Ingrid, spooning up orange sauce vigorously. 'You were a fool to miss out on this.'

'It looks delicious,' said Rachel politely. 'The point is, you *said* you knew her.'

'Beatrice Cellini? Yes. Not best pleased with young Cellini's novel, you can imagine. Would you like to meet her?'

This was so exactly what Rachel had been leading up to that she gasped.

'Might be a good idea,' said Ingrid. 'She'll know what to say to put you off.'

*   *   *

When Ingrid had scribbled down the address and phone number, Rachel stood up.

'Are you off to the ladies' room *again*?' queried Ingrid.

'Back in a moment,' said Rachel, as loudly and clearly as she could manage.

*   *   *

Ingrid would be settling the bill anyway, she persuaded herself, but she could not but feel rather rude as she took herself off down the back stairs without returning to say thank you for the splendid meal. She had thrown off her pursuers but their presence was puzzling. What could she discover, after all, that was not already hinted at in the novel?

CHAPTER EIGHT

Emanuel Cellini answered the door himself. He was a young man of no more than twenty-nine but whatever beauty he had possessed as an adolescent had left him altogether. His face was as smooth as if a layer beneath the skin had removed the least line of expression; the globe of his chin as hairless as a baby. He was wearing small, circular glasses and when he took them off his round eyes looked

142

unprotected and puzzled.

'The phone went all morning,' he said. I kept thinking it must be you, ringing to cancel.'

His small mouth looked prepared for snub and disappointment.

'I wouldn't do that,' she exclaimed.

He invited her in with the formality of someone who rarely has visitors, and Rachel followed him down the corridor into his living room. If he had bodyguards, she saw no sign of them.

* * *

The flat went back the distance of several rooms. She had expected something baroque and splendid, since the exterior of the house was so ornate. There were no paintings, however, and few ornaments of any kind apart from a simple travelling clock on the mantelpiece and a plain mirror; so little sign of individual habitation indeed that it might have been a room in a hotel. On the far wall of the room she made out small sepia photographs of moorland and horses, heather and castle, a graceful woman in a long dress fringed at the hem; another, in an art deco, head-hugging hat; a man with an early motor car.

'May I?' she asked, approaching to look at them.

Far from finding her curiosity an intrusion, his face lit up.

'My family. Well, I don't *know* the English ones, though I've found out who they are. Look, this is my great uncle. An English milord. Do you recognise him?'

'They all look rather like that when they go on a shoot,' she said. 'I had an Uncle William . . .'

'You could be a relation,' he said.

She laughed, a little uncertainly, standing in front of the blown-up, real-life photograph of a graceful woman wearing the nipped-in New Look dress of the post-war period.

'And this is your mother?'

He nodded.

'Lovely, isn't she?'

*   *   *

He offered her a chair, and a little clumsily brought out gin, lemon and tonic, which she accepted. She noticed that he seemed reluctant to meet her gaze as he spoke, but it was shyness rather than shiftiness, she decided, and almost engaging; an adolescent ungainliness.

'You live very *tidily*,' she observed.

His eyes met hers for only a moment before turning away.

'Yes. I like clear surfaces. Especially in this room. It makes me feel peaceful. And I don't work in here, or read.'

'Or watch television? Play records?' She

144

looked around.

'When I feel low, music is the only thing that gets through. More than words. Far more. Don't you ever feel like that?'

She remembered the singer who had once been his tutor.

'Would you like to hear some? Mozart, Bach, or something modern?'

'Now?'

'You could come and see my music room. I spend most of my time there.'

*   *   *

Emanuel led her along the corridor, matter-of-factly pointing out on the way an open door through which she could see a cinema screen. and a single deep chair.

'I don't go out much,' he explained.

'Do you watch videos?'

'I prefer film,' he said.

'You don't entertain?'

'I see very few people.'

She wondered who they would be, but did not ask him. He had begun to talk without her prompting, and it seemed foolish to check the flow.

*   *   *

A little further down the same corridor, a black door opened onto the music room.

145

Rachel had been expecting a piano, grace and beauty; instead there was a computer, a huge power tower of memory, and a digital keyboard.

'This is where I compose,' he said.

'So you write music, too.'

'It is *all* I write for myself,' he said gravely. 'Would you like to listen?'

'Of course,' she said, though her heart sank a little at the thought of the likely noises from another planet.

He smiled.

'It's quiet music.'

*   *   *

A tape whirred and began. A tune sung as if by a blackbird was joined by a single flute and the gentle beat of a cello.

'It's lovely,' she said, surprised.

'Yes?' He began to explain how he achieved his effects and, though his face shone for a moment with pleasure at her praise, she thought it was as much pride in the technology as in anything he had done.

'Do you want to see my study? The music will follow us in there. I couldn't work without it.'

Once again, she obeyed him, careful to say nothing that would block this unexpected flow of confidence.

'The study is the heart of my life, of course. And I'm lucky. It's very large, isn't it? And I like to watch the trees all year round through the windows: beech trees, willows; there's cherry blossom in spring. Sometimes I find it hard to believe that buses are trundling by at the other side of the house. Even here, the noise of the traffic is kept away by the fringe of cypress trees.'

There was something odd about the cadence of his voice. Not the accent. Not the intonation. Something she recognised but couldn't place.

'Do you like to live alone?' she asked.

'I don't feel as if I'm alone. Her photograph keeps me company.'

Her skin rippled for a moment with alarm, and once again he seemed altogether unaware of it. His fringed eyes found hers for another quick glance before looking away, and then he began to speak in a kind of rush.

'There's usually someone in at night either below me or above me, so I don't have to be scared.'

It wasn't what she had meant, and she said so.

'I see. *Yes*, then. I *like* being alone. It's free. Especially that funny moment of freedom over breakfast, just before you start work. I like not having to interact with people. I don't enjoy having to make conversation. Maybe it's unnatural.'

'Not even with friends? Good friends?'

He shook his head.

*   *   *

She wondered whether they were having a conversation at that moment. Probably not. He had decided what to say before she arrived, and was saying no more than he intended. The puzzle was only why he wanted to say it to her.

'What *do* you enjoy? Apart from music, I mean?'

'Puzzles. Games. I like to surf the net. I have email friends,' he remembered. 'I forgot to say that.'

*   *   *

She had followed him to a room across the corridor as white as the first, though much more attractive because three tall windows formed one wall, and through them came all the colours of a town garden. He had arranged the desk underneath those windows, and on the desktop stood an Apple Mac computer, with a screensaver of an intricate abstract design of interweaving circles. There were no piles of papers, no sign of a writing life. It was rather disconcerting. Bookshelves covered three walls from floor to ceiling, all the books

148

set neatly in their appointed places. Fiction and poetry, for the most part, she observed, in alphabetical order, naturally, and including a large number of English books. Among them, she saw with surprise and gratification, five of her father's novels arranged in order of publication.

'You keep your books meticulously,' said Rachel.

'I have a great fear of disorder. It's always there, isn't it, chaos, ready to wash in and take over everything? The second law of thermodynamics: entropy.'

He gave her another quick, shy look, and then away again.

'I was never much good at science when I was at school,' she admitted. 'Not after O Level, anyway. I'm sorry now.'

'It's the rigour I like. Physics, maths and chemistry. For a time at university, I read computer studies.'

'What happened?' she asked.

'I took a degree.' He had lost interest in the matter. 'These days I keep to a routine. Get up at six, summer and winter; work for an hour or two; walk down the streets; take coffee at the same café. I like that.'

'You don't find it a bit inflexible? As an artist?' she asked him, but saw at once that it was quite the wrong thing to say.

'But I'm not an artist.'

'I don't just mean your music,' she said

quickly, thinking he had misunderstood. 'I meant your writing, your wonderful novel . . . Can we talk about that?'

'The novel is only a kind of ventriloquism,' he said abruptly.

She was puzzled.

'Then whose is the voice?'

Again, his eyes flew away from hers.

'And the music is only therapy. I'm no artist. I haven't the temperament, you see. Or the feeling. I never had that kind of humanity. Think of the novel as a kind of service I perform. Like a translator. The exact analogy. My work is a kind of translation. Don't you understand?'

She was trying to fumble a story together, but he stood up restlessly, as if disappointed by the slowness of her response.

*　　　*　　　*

On a flat, plain table there was a simple black and white chess board, set out with an endgame. She stared at it, trying to find a way into the puzzle. Her own son was a good player, but she had never had much talent herself. He, too, stared for a moment, as if running through a number of possibilities.

'I saw Kasparov was defeated by a computer after all,' she said brightly, as a means of conversation, since he appeared to have forgotten her altogether in his concentration on the board.

'Hmm?' he said, not hearing her words and drawn completely inwards.

'Kasparov,' she repeated. 'Were you interested in his games with a computer? I read about them a few months ago. In a newspaper.'

He lifted his head and seemed to focus on the key word in her sentence.

'Kasparov? Yes, I played him once,' he said indifferently. 'It was only a simultaneous display, of course.'

*   *   *

He motioned her to follow him back into another white room, smaller than the study, where she saw a modest meal had been set out on the dining table, carefully covered with cloths against possible contamination by insects. Once again the neatness and precision of the arrangements struck her.

'Do you have a servant?' she enquired.

'Absolutely not,' he said. 'I can't bear to be overlooked. In any way. That's one of the pleasures of living on the second floor. I don't have to draw my curtains. The windows are too high for me to be seen from the gardens, too far away from the houses on the other side for anyone to make out my doings.'

'And what *are* your doings?' Rachel asked, and then quickly added, as she saw a line

151

appear between his black eyebrows, 'By which I mean what are you working on?'

'As I say, I work at translation,' he said. 'Always translation. It is all I do well. The music I played you is for my own joy only. I don't think of it as work.'

He spoke very quickly, and this time she had a sense the answer had been rehearsed. And of course that was the strangeness of the tone. He was speaking of something already written.

She accepted a chair at the table, and found herself asking why, if he so hated seeing people, he had decided to see her.

He seemed to hesitate.

'We shall come to that. You have met my father. As you've gathered, he and I don't get on. Never have. But then, I get on with so few people, it may not be his fault. Since the novel was published, we haven't met. I know what he says about me. I don't care about that.'

And suddenly she saw beauty in his face; a flash of the delicate boy that she had imagined after reading the novel.

'The point is, I don't want you to write about my mother from his point of view.'

*   *   *

She was embarrassed. He looked so defenceless, so vulnerable. Was she trying to cheat him into revealing his innermost being? There were limits to treachery in the name of earning a crust. Nothing could be more disgusting than betraying this gentle creature. She was intrigued; she was curious; but she didn't follow up the invitation to question him. Instead, she began to speak eagerly about how much she liked the novel, of her interest in Seneca, about the attraction of the Phaedra story.

'I don't know anything about Phaedra,' he said.

'I don't mean the incest theme,' she said, missing the oddity of his reply for a moment and continuing with her own thoughts. 'The lovers are not *related* in your novel, are they? Not even perceived to be, as they would have been by the Greeks. The taboo is the love between a woman in her twenties and a much younger boy. Fourteen, isn't he? What makes it strange is your story deals with a *successful* seduction. And that is altogether different from the classical tellings. And all the modern ones. In Euripides the tragedy is brought on by Hippolytus' *refusal* to acknowledge the power of sexual love. It's the revenge of a goddess to madden poor Phaedra with lust. There's never any question of Hippolytus yielding, is there? How did you come to make such a profound change?'

'I can't answer you,' he said levelly. 'The boy is young, and desperately lonely.'

*   *   *

153

A hundred questions crowded to her mind and she dismissed each in turn. He spoke of the novel as if it had been born fully formed within him.

'You have a great interest in English literature,' she began again. 'I see from your books.'

'Yes. My mother left me her library. I spoke the language as a child and I studied English again to understand her. It seems to be one of the skills I have, learning languages. I do it by rote, of course; from tapes and books. I have no true facility.'

He *wanted* her to ask about his mother. He was bored with her other questions. It was not her fault then, if she continued to probe.

'About your mother, then,' she asked. 'Your father must have been very distressed when she died.'

'He said she was mad. That she jumped because she was mad.'

As he did not go on, she prompted him.

'To be kidnapped must be very alarming. The novel doesn't explain how you were rescued. Do you remember anything about that? I know you were only very small . . .'

'If I was kidnapped,' he said. 'Perhaps my father locked me in the cellar for a few days. Just to teach me some kind of lesson.'

'But you *must* know,' she exclaimed. 'It's your history. Your life. Well, your *novel* anyway.'

'You don't understand in the least, do you? It's *her* pain I care about. I don't feel I inhabit my life,' he said. 'I just observe it, really. Always have. I live on its margin. I don't expect you to make anything of that.'

She said slowly, 'I sometimes look at my own stupid behaviour, if that's what you mean, as if at someone else. That's quite normal, I suspect.'

'I don't know about what's normal. I doubt I ever was. As a child I was pretty dysfunctional, ill for a great deal of the time. They thought there was something wrong with my heart and I was put in hospital. They put a probe down an artery to look. They said I was very brave but, you know, it was like watching a programme on television.'

'How old were you?'

'Oh, I don't know. Maybe nine.'

She remembered her own son's childish terror of hospital.

'Don't you think you were brave?'

He shook his head. 'No, because I wasn't afraid.'

'Other children *would* have been afraid.'

'I never know what other people feel,' he said plaintively. 'I don't know what you feel now.'

'But of *course* you do. You write so brilliantly of other people's inner worlds.'

'No,' he said impatiently. 'I've already

155

explained.'

Now he lifted his eyes to meet hers, as if he knew that only by holding her gaze with his own could he persuade her of the importance of what he was saying. She was startled by the intensity of his words, but at first she did not have their measure. He shook his head impatiently.

'You think I understand the novel, but I don't. It's a collage of voices,' he said. 'I think of them as *remembered* voices. I don't understand what it is about, what it could mean. That is why I give no interviews.'

There was nothing menacing in the boy's gentle face but he did not sound entirely sane either.

He had begun to frighten her a little.

'So why see me, then?' she asked directly.

'I already told you,' he said.

'You want me to see *her* point of view,' she remembered slowly. 'I see.'

'My mother read a great many English writers,' he continued, quite unaware of her apprehension. 'You will see them round the walls of my study. That is all I have of her, that and her papers. I was given both when I was twenty-one.'

'Yes,' she said.

'The library included some novels by your dead father,' he said. 'He was a writer she much admired.'

'How can you know, apart from that one

156

epigraph?' she asked.

'She made notes in the books. Naturally. If you like, I will show you her annotations. In some of his books she had written many times in the margin: *Marvellous.* Does that please you?'

'It astonishes me. And, yes, I am pleased. Which one do you think she liked most?'

'It was a book about Ancient Rome. About a corrupt politician.'

'Of course,' she said, 'I am proud that my father's work was so valued.'

'I don't really know why she *did* admire that particular book,' he frowned. 'I have read it several times. I take very little interest in politics. I suppose I was looking for images of my father.'

'Perhaps he is there in the doubleness of the politician?' she suggested. 'The one who wanted to do so much good, and could only damage everyone he loved.'

He shook his head impatiently.

'I think she would have liked me to see you. You have kept the same name as your father,' he said, with a fleeting expression of pleasure on his face. 'I'm glad. You are even quite like him, to judge from the photograph on the jacket. But you understand nothing.'

He began to pull at his ear-lobe, a gesture he had made many times before, she could see.

*   *   *

She risked another question.

'Tell me about your stepmother?'

He said nothing, but his shrug of disappointment showed she had lost his interest altogether.

'A friend of mine speaks well of her,' she explained.

'My father had his marriage annulled,' he said. 'I have not seen her since then.'

They had finished their salads. He rose, stacked the plates neatly together.

'Excuse me. I must clear away.'

*   *   *

She could hear from the kitchen that he was already washing them by hand. It was almost as if he were washing her inept questions away. Rachel hoped she had not upset him. She had no wish to disturb him further. She almost wanted to mother him, to hold him safe, to console him. She was hot and tired now and had begun to hear in her head the beat of her own blood like a drum.

*   *   *

'You have been generous,' she called into the kitchen. 'I wonder if there is anything you would like me to do for you in return? Perhaps you have other work. I am sure the whole world would be fascinated.'

There is no more work of mine,' he called back. 'I don't *want* there to be any more. Ever. It's enough.'

Then he appeared at the door, looking white and ill.

'I *never* wanted to be a writer. It gives me no pleasure. It was my *mother* who wanted to write. And no one is interested in that. Even you. You don't ask to see her work,' he accused her.

'I didn't know anything about it,' she said. 'Naturally, I'm interested.'

'I'm hardly a judge,' he said impatiently. 'All I know is what I have already told you. She wanted to write; it was the passion of her life. She lived like a white bird who is not allowed to fly.'

'*Would* you let me see her work?' Rachel asked tentatively.

He had become very agitated.

'I don't want you to carry it away and put it down in your room when you get back to London and forget about it.'

'I won't do that.'

She laughed, in an attempt to reduce the tension which was now apparent in the line of his shoulders and the cords of his neck.

'You could make a copy,' he said. 'But you are a busy woman. A journalist.'

'I'm not *really* a journalist,' she said. 'And I promise I will read it. I won't take it away without making a copy.'

*   *   *

She was heartbreakingly sorry for the boy.
When he returned, she had a momentary
impulse to soothe him, as she would have
soothed Tom long ago when something at
school had upset him, but she saw all
Emanuel's attention was now on the bulky
packets he was carrying.

'In the manilla envelope is a kind of
journal,' he said. 'I can't read it. I don't
understand it. Don't look at it now. Not here.
But take it away.'

'What do you want me to do with it?'

'I have a responsibility. To her. That's why I
want you here. I want you to help me.'

'I'll do anything I can.'

'But—two things, then. First. My father
must *never* hear of this.'

'I . . .'

'He mustn't know you have read what I am
going to give you. Do you promise?'

She hesitated.

'It would be dangerous for *you*,' he said. 'I
am thinking of you.'

Better not to use the hotel Xerox machine
then, she thought.

'I promise.'

'You can write about it. I *want* you to write
about it. He will do nothing to me. But don't

160

mention the journals.'

'That might be tricky,' she frowned.

'My editor—' she began.

'Look. I *want* you to write about my mother. It is my price for the interview, you see. Do you follow me now?'

She hoped she did not. The intensity in his face appalled her.

'I have stolen her spirit,' he muttered. 'It is all her voice. All I did was to transcribe her words to me.'

Her skin prickled uneasily. He spoke as if he had direct communication with his mother's ghost. She was still sorry for him but, if he believed what he was saying, he had to be completely mad.

'I will do what I can,' said Rachel, doubtfully.

*   *   *

Back at the hotel, it was by no means clear what she should do or what she wanted to do. The triumph she had felt earlier at getting the interview was disappearing as she imagined introducing a paragraph that would please Emanuel into a piece intended for the worldly eyes of Ridley Martin. Rachel drew back from the thought. She would have to be very careful. Some of the largest publishers in the world would be ready to slap down writs against any article hinting Emanuel was still in touch with his dead mother, that he was *literally* a ghost writer. Even Pontius Pilate could not have felt more inclined to wash his hands of the whole enterprise.

*   *   *

And there was another problem. She had seen no obvious minders as she left Emanuel's flat. Still, she had taken the precaution of concealing the files in a copy of *Corriere della Sera*. Where could she leave them now? The hotel safe was clearly open to any of Cellini's minions who wanted to search it, and they might well do so if they knew she had visited Emanuel. The packet was too bulky to carry about. One envelope was marked with her name and she took that out, folded it and put it away in her bag. The only person she felt she could really trust was Joshua, whatever Ingrid said about him.

*   *   *

She decided to speak to him from the lobby of the Hilton on the way to see Beatrice Cellini. As she expected, he was a little grumpy.

'I thought you'd gone very quiet. What have you been up to?'

'Come down a moment and I'll tell you,' she said. 'I've got a taxi outside.'

'Going *where*?' he asked suspiciously.

162

She told him she had an appointment with Beatrice Cellini, and that seemed to mollify him.

'But I want to leave something with you,' she explained. 'I'll just keep the envelope addressed to me. The rest . . .'

'I'll sit on whatever it is like an egg,' he promised.

She did not confess she had already arranged to break her word about Giorgio.

*   *   *

Beatrice's apartment was expensively but outlandishly furnished, with pink satin curtains, crimson cushions, huge bulbous chairs, and sofas that could have been used as double beds. The combination of pinks and reds gave the whole room an odd texture reminiscent of human flesh. Yet, for all the vulgarity, there was a kind of exuberance in the décor.

*   *   *

Beatrice Cellini herself bore a striking resemblance to a plumper, rather sluttish Marlene Dietrich. She was lying on a couch in a housecoat slit to reveal one leg to the thigh. Her fluffy mules, kicked off on the carpet, had two-inch heels. Her beauty was the flamboyant kind that looks best on stage: high cheekbones, ice-chip blue eyes, heavily marked lashes. Those eyes now assessed Rachel.

'Come in, my dear,' she said, in the tone of voice Marlene Dietrich herself might have used to an unfortunate starlet chosen to play a foil to her own glamour. 'I have to say you look nothing like Ingrid.'

'Why on earth should I?' asked Rachel, startled.

'Ingrid said there was some kind of family connection. I was intrigued.'

'She was my father's literary agent,' said Rachel crisply. 'He was a novelist.'

Beatrice's manner, voice and posture were so studied that Rachel felt a momentary surge of dislike for the woman who had obviously never heard of Frank O'Malley.

The fine eyebrows rose.

'I see. How disappointing.'

She gave a sudden, surprising giggle. 'Oh dear. And I'm afraid, whatever you've read about my divorce settlement, I'm practically penniless. I never could hold on to money. I wonder what Ingrid was thinking of?'

'I'm not *asking* for money,' said Rachel, reddening.

'Then how else can I help? Do pull that switch, will you? Don't you find the blinds have to come down at this time in the evening? My eyes ache, otherwise.'

They looked clear and sharp to Rachel. She stood up and followed the languidly extended arm to the far wall, and the blinds made a silent, electronic descent.

* * *

'I wanted to ask you a few questions.'

'I see. A journalist. Well, I'd like to be helpful, but I don't think I really can. If it's about my former husband, I've *nothing* to tell you. I never knew anything about his business affairs. And if I *knew* anything, can you imagine I would be so foolish as to talk about it?'

'I haven't come to talk about Giorgio,' Rachel began with incautious familiarity.

Beatrice picked up the use of the first name immediately. Her blue eyes gave a knowing twinkle, and she smiled.

'So. What then?'

'I wondered if you would say something about your stepson.'

'Don't wonder. I won't.'

'Did you see much of him when he was growing up?'

'You think you can bullshit *me*?' asked Beatrice, incredulously. 'It's that filthy novel, isn't it?'

Rachel flushed.

'You want to know if I taught him how to fuck. Isn't that right? That's what the book is saying. Jesus Maria, another woman would have sued. Even I could have sued. I could

165

have taken out an injunction.'

'So why didn't you?' asked Rachel quickly.

Beatrice stared at her in surprise for a moment and then began to laugh aloud at the impudence. It was a wonderful, chortling laugh, which brought a flashing merriment to the brilliant eyes.

'Think about it. Someone like me going to law. Can't you imagine what a time they'd have, the barristers on the other side?'

She laughed again, lowering her head as she did so and looking up through her hair at Rachel, like a mischievous child delighted at her own insights.

'You don't *do* that, do you, with a history like mine? Unless you are *very* stupid. Think of the character witnesses they would call. I've always wondered about Oscar Wilde, you know. I suppose he thought he could use the courtroom as a kind of theatre. There'd be no excuse for me, making a mistake like that. I've been in courts before, and I know what goes on.' She laughed again. *'Might* have been amusing, I suppose. I can just see the judge bending over to look down my cleavage and asking *"Where* did you say you got an education, my girl?" But in any case, Giorgio advised me not to.'

'I bet he did,' said Rachel.

'Meaning?'

'He wouldn't have wanted the case all over the papers.'

166

'I really think you believe it, don't you? That Emanuel's novel is about me? Jesus Maria.'

'I didn't say that.'

With a little flick, Beatrice turned the spot of the lamp at her side onto Rachel's face.

'How did you meet Giorgio?'

'At a party,' said Rachel primly.

'One of those dreary political affairs, with dressed-up wives and everybody so *bored* they're glad to go home at nine?' Beatrice laughed again. 'Oh dear. Men are disgraceful, aren't they? Touching you up while the canapes go round. You enjoyed it, I expect. Well, you would, wouldn't you? So *flattering.*'

'We talked,' said Rachel crossly. That's all.'

She felt she was being invited into a wicked complicity.

'But that's what we *need,* isn't it?' Beatrice sighed. 'It's always the words that turn us on, the pleasure of being desired. Which is why marriage is so much less sexy than a one-night stand. Have you tried marriage?'

'As it happens, I *was* married for a time,' said Rachel reluctantly.

'Dull in comparison, don't you agree? When it isn't *worse*. Mind you, I don't think women should live alone. I'm not a feminist. Are you?'

'Yes, I am,' said Rachel. 'Even if it isn't fashionable any more. Do you feel Giorgio treated you as an equal?'

Rachel was hoping to nudge Beatrice into giving her a new lead. Then she need barely refer to what Emanuel had been saying, simply describe his apartment. She had to feed Ridley something. Journalism, she reflected, is a treacherous profession,

'Giorgio always felt he was entirely in the right, whoever he was dealing with. Men usually do, especially when they're fucking you over.'

'Your English is surprisingly colloquial,' said Rachel.

'When I was young,' said Beatrice, 'I lived in New York for a while. It's hardly an accomplishment. Everybody speaks English now.' Beatrice pursed her lips, as if in thought. 'I think you must have seen Emanuel, already. How did you get to him? He tries so hard to hide away. And for the most part Giorgio protects him. Oh yes, he keeps people like you away usually.'

She paused, and then began to speak very rapidly, with an unconvincing nonchalance.

'Did Emanuel mention me? Not that I care what he says. But I wondered. Of course we don't meet now. But perhaps?'

Rachel met the glittering blue eyes full on, and for the first time in the entire conversation watched Beatrice's gaze drop.

'I don't think he spoke of you,' said Rachel,

after a pause. 'He spoke of his mother. And his own concerns.'

'Which don't include *me*. Yes, I understand. Thank you.'

There was a pause. Beatrice looked genuinely upset. For the first time since she had let Rachel into the room, her voice sounded entirely natural.

'Have you ever tried to make friends with the child of a married man? When you love the man?'

As it happens, Rachel had, at the secret heart of her last love affair, met a small, angry child out shopping with his father and for one afternoon tried to interest him in Regent's Park Zoo. She nodded.

'It's not so easy, is it?' said Beatrice quietly. 'It is hard to be a stepmother to a sensitive boy. I don't know why. Stepfathers are more abusive, whatever the fairy tales tell us. Look in the newspapers. Sometimes a battered woman will collude in terrible things, but it's not so common. And yet we are the ones who are hated.'

Rachel had an intuition that, rather as Emanuel had, Beatrice would continue speaking if she said nothing. Any question would remind her of the presence of a stranger. She fell silent.

'When children disappear, the stepfather is responsible again and *again*. The men *look* so heartbroken on television, but it's usually an act, isn't it? They beat the children they have not fathered; especially boys. It's biology. When the girls are pretty, men fondle them, and sometimes more. But when a mother dies, a second wife has the hardest time of any. Because she is competing with a ghost. A usurper cannot expect to be loved. But you don't believe in ghosts?'

'Not in general,' said Rachel.

'Sometimes I do,' said Beatrice. 'I'm a village girl, you see. We are very superstitious.'

*   *   *

In the gentle half-light, the hardness had gone from Beatrice's eyes and lips as she began to talk, almost as if to herself.

'Perhaps I damaged him. I've never been sure whether my need for friendship was what tipped him over. Or whether we helped one another; two lonely people.'

She paused, as if for a question, but Rachel went on waiting.

'One long summer, I was locked away like a princess in a castle, burning with energy. The streets of Rome would have saved me, but I could find no way to return there. If I raised the telephone from its hook, I could hear the fat cook breathing on the extension by day, and the servant by night. Sometimes I heard songs, violins and gaiety coming from the village, but no servant could be bribed to let me out. The palazzo was my prison. I didn't understand why it had to be like that and why Giorgio wasn't there. It wasn't money I married him for: I expected him to be with me. Instead I was stuck out in the country like a *wife*. I was not meant to be a wife. So, after a time, I grew crafty. Do you understand me?

*   *   *

Rachel nodded warily.

'I see you do, but let me explain. I'm a street child. His servants knew me well, those peasants. Perhaps they pitied me. Remember, I was only twenty-five. They recognised the sickness, and they watched me. All day I felt a pounding in my throat and my ears. Sometimes I threw off my dress and let the sun brown my whole body. They guessed I was no longer waiting for a husband's return. Sometimes it was Piero I longed for. Or the man who handled the dogs.'

*   *   *

This was going to turn into a confession. Rachel tried to conceal her excitement, but Beatrice seemed to pick up on the movement of her thoughts.

'Don't be foolish,' she said wearily. 'I felt no lust for Emanuel. The mind of every young boy is filled with lecherous thoughts. It is

171

natural. In his case, it became a sickness, like a curse. And shall I tell you why the fiction has to be a complete lie? Exactly why that novel is complete bullshit? Because I had no children of my own. Now think about that,' said Beatrice. 'Have you any children?'

'I have a son,' said Rachel, with the usual pang of anxiety.

'Well, I was not so fortunate. And not for lack of trying. It was because of what some foul gynaecologist did to me when I was seventeen. Just before I met Giorgio. He would have seen I was properly looked after, but in those days I had no choices. My dear, can you imagine how tenderly I felt towards a child in my care? How far my emotions were from those he imagined?'

'I *think* I can,' said Rachel, uncertainly.

'I tried to show him all my wasted maternal affection. Can you understand that?' she asked Rachel.

'Of course I do,' said Rachel.

The pause lengthened. Whatever Beatrice was remembering, she was not speaking of it. Rachel realised she would have to risk questioning her.

'So you went to Emanuel's room at night?' she asked, and then, as the glittering eyes came back into focus to stare at her, she added hastily, 'I remember doing the same when I was lonely. You were saying you were lonely.'

'All I wanted was to look at the tenderness

172

of his lips and face. His skin had barely a pore, you know. He was a child. Only a child. He had all the unblemished beauty of childhood. I don't know what he felt about me. Probably my affection was love poured into the sand like blood. Whatever his thoughts, I took the comfort that a loved child gives his mother. I had no child of my own. Is it my fault that he constructs this pornography? I wonder sometimes if the whole story is only a kind of dream. An account of how he *wishes* it had been. You read of that, don't you? False memories. Therapists construct them for their patients, patients invent them to please their therapists. Who knows how he came to invent his story, poor boy, poor boy. Do you think it could be some vengeance his mother's ghost took upon me?'

'It's not an idea I would have,' said Rachel uneasily.

'Poor dead woman. I wished her no harm.'

There was a pause.

'How does he look? Is he still thin and pale?'

'No,' said Rachel. 'I would say he is rather overweight.'

'No way. Impossible,' said Beatrice, blinking.

'You haven't seen him for many years,' Rachel reminded her. She felt she must press her advantage. 'If what you say is true, how did you and Giorgio come to separate?'

'Oh, my dear, that is another story. He treated me well enough. Considering.'

'Considering what?'

'Well, considering my behaviour. And what his first wife had been.' Beatrice laughed. 'The angel of the house, you know.'

'You knew her then?' said Rachel.

'Hardly. People don't, do they? Get to know sick wives. I'm not sure I'm the right person to ask. Second wives aren't charitable. But, if you want my opinion, she was mean and jealous.'

'Didn't she have reason to be?'

'No. She was jealous for something she had no use for. She should have lived as a spinster, walking about some Scottish hillside with a dog. The life would have suited her. She might have been healthier.'

'You obviously didn't like her,' said Rachel.

'I don't even know how she came to summon the *energy* to jump.'

'It wasn't an accident, then?'

'Her brain must have been turned.'

'By the kidnap?'

'I know nothing about it.'

'Do you know who was responsible?'

'Who knows all Giorgio's enemies? As God's my witness. Perhaps I should have asked Maria. But I never did.'

'You mean there really *was* a servant called Maria?'

'My dear, every Sicilian woman has Maria in her name. You are a stranger to Italy.'

174

Beatrice was sitting up, shaking her hair over her shoulders. She looked at her watch. Rachel saw she was to be dismissed soon, and asked urgently, 'What is there to cover up, do you imagine?'

'Did I say there was? No, I don't think I said that.'

'You said Cellini kept the press away.'

To protect the child. Naturally. Nothing more.'

'I don't believe it,' said Rachel. 'Look, I've been followed for days. Why? I was no danger to Emanuel. Or Cellini.'

But even as she spoke, she knew. The answer was in the papers. It had to be. She was wasting her time expecting Beatrice to divulge anything.

*   *   *

'There was no question of murder?'

'Good Lord, what a fantasy. Where would be the motive for that?'

'You wanted Giorgio. He wanted you.'

'We already *had* each other. Silly girl, he was more mine then, truly, than ever he was after we married. I see what you think. That I wanted her out of the way. But I had no need of that.'

'And Maria?'

'Giorgio brought her into his house from the streets of Sicily. She thought *all* of us

175

were interlopers.

'Did she say that?'

'I told you, we never talked. Sometimes I wish we had. And now she is dead. End of story. Or it ought to be.'

'But the story still troubles you?'

'Only the Englishwoman. She haunts me because she hated me. That's what it is. Though sometimes I wonder—'

'Yes?'

'Did she, in her misery . . . because of me— Was that what happened?' Beatrice shook her head. 'She had a small, neat mouth. A bit like yours, but tighter, more prudish. I don't think you are a prude. We can do what we like these days, can't we? Nothing is forbidden. I never wanted to hurt her. People always do harm when they take what they want . . . don't they?'

Her voice trailed away.

'Will you go now, please? I wish I had never let you in.'

*   *   *

It was in a café on the Via Veneto, sipping a Campari, that Rachel began to read the contents of the envelope Emanuel had addressed to her. It was indeed a journal, the first pages neatly written and syntactical, an account of unexpected happiness. Then the writing began to sprawl jaggedly across the page, difficult to read, desperate. Sometimes

176

single phrases only. Rachel read avidly, even when the writing was almost impossible to decipher.

CHAPTER NINE

The first few entries were written in an eager, innocent Italian that Rachel could read without problem. Then they fell into English. Rachel cast her mind back to the photograph in Emanuel's living room: the slim, perfectly dressed figure that might have come from an early Bertolucci film.

We are at the seaside. I was worried about appearing with my pregnant body distended, but our beach is so secluded I could bathe naked if I liked. The water is clean and clear and green. We make love only once, gently, because I am afraid it will hurt the baby, though Giorgio says there is no danger; and I trust him. No one could love a son more, and I know I am carrying a son. I have been told so by the hospital. He is healthy, and big, and I only have to wait.

August 5, 1970
The baby came two weeks early. My mother was in Scotland visiting my aunt. I don't blame her for that; she hates Italy in the summer; but I think she should have warned me how painful it

177

is to give birth. The books speak only of contractions and relaxing into them. For me it was a two-day buffeting by waves of pain until they decided I should have a Caesarian. I shall not want another child. Giorgio says I will feel differently soon, but I cannot imagine it. The child himself is perfect: tender-lipped, with round blue eyes like my mother and long black lashes. They say his eyes will go brown, and Giorgio hopes they will, but I don't mind. He looks like Giorgio in any case. My mother would have liked to move into our house to look after me when I return home, but Giorgio was opposed to the idea. She makes him uneasy, he says; she is so Scottish and bossy. My father says the same, but he thinks it is because she is the daughter of a duke. Giorgio has hired Maria, a good Catholic he says, to look after the baby as well as myself. She is fat and jolly and I am happy to have her near me.

August 25
Two days after going home I had a haemorrhage; I almost died. It happened about seven in the evening. Maria had just brought me lemon tea. I felt the heat rising in me suddenly, and then the blood pouring out as if my life were flowing away from me like the water running down the plug-hole bath. I was taken away on a stretcher with rubber pipes in my nose, and terror in my heart. Perhaps God was abandoning me. Because I had consulted an English doctor.

Because I wanted to cheat Giorgio of any more children. The priest said that was wicked. But it isn't wicked in England, and I can't believe God thinks it is wicked. Well, now I'm in hospital. They've put a drip into my wrist; my days are bloodless. I wait every day for Giorgio to visit me. Some days he is in Palermo. Or Milan. He says he loves me, when he appears. I don't want to die. I want to see Emanuel grow up. I already love him more than anyone in the world.

*   *   *

September 7

I am not recovering as quickly as they said I would. It's as if the light has gone out of me. I have frightening, lonely dreams. I'm lost and looking for someone, someone whose name I've forgotten. And I'm afraid to be alone. When the light goes in the evening, every evening, my heart begins to beat louder and faster, because that is when the bleeding began. I panic unless Giorgio is at home. His presence soothes me. Only his presence. I don't want to talk to him or touch him, only to know he is there. That he would save me if I bled again. At first I think he understood. Now he gets bored; he cannot sit and hold my hand; he does not like to read books, and I am too exhausted to be charming; I have nothing to say. I hold the child in my arms; his lips smell of milk.

September 15

I know what Giorgio wants from me. He asks me to feel his penis in my hands, to take it into my mouth, but the wound in my stomach still hurts even though the stitches are out. I obey him, but I'm angry. Not at the indelicacy, but the egotism. His need, always so insistent, even though I am still ill. Seeing my reluctance, he mistakes my hesitation: he promises to withdraw before he comes. Then I taste his body between my lips, and he pushes it deeper and deeper into my mouth until I begin to gag and protest. As I strain, I am afraid the wound in my belly will open. Afterwards he said he did not like my sullen expression. I know I have displeased him. A wife should want to give her husband sexual relief.

September 21

I am still frail. My weight is down to seven stone, but perhaps I am recovering. I can walk about the house now with the child in my arms; I can sing. And read. The evenings are a problem, however. Giorgio rarely comes in before nine. And sometimes he is away altogether. When I feel panic coming on, Maria looks after Emanuel. And I look out at the darkness. The reality that is the darkness. The end to which we all come. There's nothing afterwards. I know now I was close enough to that edge. Giorgio wants me to pray. He blames my English scepticism. Sometimes I show a flash of my old spirit. 'You were glad enough to ally yourself to my grand family,' I say. And then we quarrel. Last night I called him a street child, without manners or mercy. I have not seen him today.

October 27
My father comes to see me more often than my mother. He adored me once; I was the centre of the world. I am not the centre of Giorgio's world, I know that, but what then is his centre? His son, perhaps. Or his work. My father asks me what it is, this work that occupies him so much. I answer proudly that it is politics. I explain his fight against corruption. How he wants the poor to have a chance, how he understands the injustice of Italy and wants to put it right. He shakes his head. 'Politics or the Mafia, it's the same in Italy.'

My father is worried about me; he can see my heart is heavy; he thinks it is because Giorgio neglects me. He would like me, he says, to stand up for my rights. He won't interfere, however; he is too timid. He tells me Giorgio repaid the whole mortgage on the estate. That I must respect him as my husband. I explain I understand Giorgio has to go away, that his work is very demanding. I can see he wonders about those absences, wonders about whether Giorgio is looking after his daughter, whether I am happy with him. I tell him the truth: that I am only happy when

Giorgio is there, his big soft kiss on my cheek, his heavy hand on my neck. But there are things I don't tell him: that I no longer want Giorgio to make love with me; that I never want him inside me. His loving frightens me, it is so violent, so powerful, I am afraid he will pull me open and I shall bleed again and die. That we quarrel over his wish for another child.

February, 1972

Another year. I have been quietly at work on another book. And so I haven't kept my journal. No matter. Now that I am stronger, I ask questions. I am not a little street girl; I am the granddaughter of a duke. My father's name goes back to Dante. I am not afraid to speak up for myself. Where does Giorgio go when he leaves me in the morning? To the office, he used to say. But now he answers, 'I have fingers in many pies.' He is glad to leave the house, to leave me, I can see that. I would argue more, if I were more unhappy about his departure. I have become accustomed to it. One thing surprises me: now that Emanuel runs about and holds on to his legs, Giorgio is less patient with him. See he is disciplined, *he tells Maria. His mother is too indulgent to the boy. And he is right. I would give him anything. He is my only happiness.*

I know we get richer every day: there are more servants, more paintings, more gardeners, and dogs in the garden to protect our property from

182

marauders. I ask him sometimes, 'How do you find it so easy to acquire wealth? My poor father always found money ran through his fingers like water.' But he only strokes my hair. 'You have lovely hair. You don't need to think *about such things.'*

These days I read a great deal. The Italian classics, and the English poets. I know he doesn't like to see me with my head in a book.

February 20, 1972
Now for my secret. I am writing stories. I have made a discovery. Nothing gives me more pleasure than writing down what I see and feel. I get up early these days. There is frost in the garden in the early morning; when it goes, the grass becomes a different colour green, especially under the beech trees. It becomes an English green. Here the grass will go brown, for all the sprinklers, in a matter of months. Now I enjoy the cold weather. I listen to the hiss of rain on the glass. When the sun comes out, I open the windows and there is a sweet-smelling mist.

I have to ask Maria to warn the dog handlers to keep the dogs on chains. I don't like their howls, and I want to walk on the grass with Emanuel today. I love the delight he takes there, snuffling the woodsmoke smells, and laughing. Such hope he has in his face, such intelligence. I love his delicate lips, his serious eyes.

183

November, 1972

Giorgio found me writing in my other book today. I showed him some of what I had done, but he put it away impatiently. 'Only spinsters write poems,' he said. And that night when he came to my bed he entered me brutally, as if he wanted the thrust of his entry to destroy such unnatural pleasures, as if they lived where he put his penis so fiercely. Up and deep he goes, with his fingers in my back passage, and then his body pushing after them, until I scream with pain. That scream made him come and brought our lovemaking to an end. If lovemaking is what it can be called, when there is such anger in it. There was a time he found me lovely enough to caress; I remembered that the other day when I saw him fondle a Renaissance marble he had recently bought. He does not savour the curves of my body now, only any orifice of which he can make use.

January 10, 1973

A cold morning. Ice breath outside. Cold winter rain. A black world. Giorgio is away from home. The cold sunlight enters me like alcohol. Even as I write the words down, I feel a measure of exhilaration. These notebooks are something of my own. Something that doesn't need a man to approve. I can sit and play with words. I read. Novels. Especially English novels. They are my secret world. When he returns, he asks me what I

184

have done, but when I explain, he shakes his head. 'Do you think you could be mentally ill?'

January 11, 1973
I have thought about those words since. Not the possibility, but the callousness of his saying it to me. Like that. So casually. It is as if my writing were a kind of adultery. And perhaps it is. But he has no right to complain, since he no longer loves me. And for me it is the only freedom I have. My hand flies over the page as if it holds my whole spirit. I am a bird rising over the gardens, the walls mean nothing to me, the guards cannot hold me. Otherwise I live in a cage.

January 25, 1973
Yesterday his Mercedes took me to visit my mother; she is dying. My father's distress was overwhelming. But when I looked down at my poor mother I thought only: 'So, you're finished, then.' I was ashamed at such a callous thought. But I've pondered it since. I was thinking of myself. Of what no longer seemed important. I remember when I was so frightened of death; now it seems natural. Like sleep. Because there is Emanuel. I shall leave behind someone who has all the best of me in him. These nights I take him in my bed and hold him close to me. A great happiness fills me, just to feel his tender body against mine.

April, 1973

Maria says she is worried Emanuel is not behaving like a normal child. He can read, but he does not chatter. Let him read, I say. He spends all his time alone, she complains. Let him, I say. If that makes him happy. And he is not alone; we are happy together. I have taught him the name of the trees; he watches their spring as seriously as I do. We keep fish in a little pool; we give them names. At night I read him stories or sing to him. And when I work, or what I call work, he plays with the gardener's boy.

September, 1973

My father has been lonely since my mother died. I remember how happy he looked at my wedding in his grey top hat and morning coat. When he visits, his unhappiness upsets me. There is something he wants to tell me. At last he gets it out. He is going to marry again. I understand. So I am alone now in a new way, except for a three-year-old boy sitting seriously in his bed and comforting a mother in tears. What could he understand?

October 12, 1973

These days, when Giorgio comes home, he does not come alone. There are men with loud voices. Their voices are rough, Sicilian, but they are not the poor whom Giorgio once wanted to protect. I know that because they are dressed in such expensively cut suits; their ties are hand-painted

186

silk. They are very polite, but they frighten me. And then there is Beatrice.

This week Beatrice has been here three times; she is part of a game played without me in another part of the house. Is she beautiful? I can't tell. I'd have to scrub off her face and strip her feathers and sequins to be sure. One day I asked Maria, 'What kind of woman is she?'

And she said, 'Forgive me, Signora. She must be a girl from a brothel.'

It may be so, but I see more confidence in her than such women have. People who are paid to please do not often carry themselves so proudly. The men are in awe of her. Of course I hate *her, whoever she is and whatever she does.*

October 18, 1973
'Who is she, Giorgio?' I asked him. 'Who is she?'

'She is someone's girl. You can see what she is.'

'Why does she come to the house?'

'They like her to come. It calms them down.'

'And do you like *her?'*

'Women like her are always necessary.'

'Does your business *involve the use of people like her?'*

'Why do you need to know about my business?'

'I am not a fool,' I cried to him, wanting to beat my wrists against his chest and force him to attend to me.

187

'No. But you are sick. Your voice is too shrill. You will alarm the child.'

'I would not harm a hair of his head.'

'Maria says he will speak to no one but you. That you are making him strange. I am worried about him.'

July 20, 1974

There is a contemporary English novelist I admire; sometimes he writes about the country houses of my grandfather's England, but he writes best of Ancient Rome, of how little has changed since the corruption of Seneca. Rome he sees as the true image of a modern city, drawing the homeless and hopeless from out of a village life of decent, family rules into hot slums and streets where everything is permitted. Giorgio has risen from those streets. He has such fine ideals, but when I try to talk to him he is impatient with me, saying I don't understand the world of politics.

August, 1974

Now the worst thing has happened. Maria and Emanuel have gone to the sea without me because Giorgio says I am ill and must stay at home. Or was it that Emanuel is ill? This morning I am confused. The doctor has come again; I hear his voice and Giorgio's outside my room. There is medicine to take. First the little yellow pills. Then the black ones. I don't write any more, except to scribble here. The pills have taken away the possibility of doing anything.

August 14, 1974
I understand now, and I am mutinous. First I refused the pills, but that was foolish. Now I pretend to be docile, put them into my mouth and hold them under my tongue. I take them out when no one is looking. I write in the moonlight, when they imagine I am sleeping. It is like a fever. I only break off to look out at the garden and watch the shadows move over the grass. I describe the rain hissing in the trees. I write conversation, too; phrases exchanged and forgotten, overheard and only now understood. I know now Giorgio's money comes from the poor and unhappy who use cocaine. It is power he loves and, whatever ideals he has, whatever good things he hopes to bring about, he gives the orders and death follows, wherever he commands. Even into the Holy City itself.

Of course I no longer allow Maria to see me write. Every night I hide my two books carefully in a locked chest; the key is on a charm bracelet on my wrist. To Maria I babble about my mother's jewels, and she helps me wrap all my other rings and bracelets in tissue paper. After my death, Emanuel will have the casket and the bracelet with the rest of my estate. During the day I sleep, and they think it is because of the drugs they have given me.

189

And why do I think of death? I am no longer afraid of it. I have made another discovery. The powder itself.

September, 1974
Beatrice often comes to the house. Even in my remoteness, even in my euphoria, I know what is happening. I have seen the way they look at each other. I have watched their exchange of smiles. Sometimes, not often, we eat together. I watch her. She is eager to be alone with him. And what then? Does she take off her clothes and lie by him so he can put a hand inside her, then his thick penis, so that she can arch back and sigh? With pleasure?

I don't need to ask him about it. What could I say?
'How can you be jealous of something you do not want yourself?' he will ask me. And he is right. 'But where is my son?' I ask him. 'Tell me that.'

January 5, 1975
If only he would let me have the car. I drive well. Even now I could. The streets would roll shinily under my wheels like the air in a dream. It would be like flying. I could drive down to the sea where there are sulphide lights and orange flares on the wet streets; I could enjoy floating in the lights. But he will not let me have the car. He will not let me leave the gardens.

January 30, 1975
I thought nothing would change. But what I meant was that nothing would get better; I had forgotten things can always get worse. Now I know it is the doctors *who have decided I should not see my son. They say I am dangerous to him. To* him. *To my son! I would die for him. And they let that whore put her hands on him freely. I have told Giorgio of my desolation.*

'Take anyone you like and let them have your body, but don't let them touch my son,' I plead with him.

He only speaks of medicine, of new medicine.

*   *   *

January 5, 1976
The white powder is blessed by the Lord. Who had the kindness to find something so powerful? It was Maria who offered it to me, when she found me weeping.

'Do you know the name of this white powder, Maria?'

'It is not my business to know names, Signora.'

But I know. And I laugh to think I once believed it wicked to deal in cocaine. Now I understand it is unhappiness *that is wicked, not the dream, not the dream. In the dream I see Emanuel. For hours I watch him growing up. For days at a time. I watch what happens to him.*

191

It is not like a daydream, where I can control what I see. No, it unrolls unpredictably, like a vision. I feel every triumph and terror clearly, as if from another planet, but always clearly. And still at night I can find my pen and write.

I write down what I dream. Then I go up to the terrace and look down. It is freezing. I could fly across the trees if I want. But I don't want to fly away. I won't *leave my son. I won't have them chase me away from him. He needs me. He needs me more than he needs his father. One night he found his own way to my bed. He had stolen there from the very far side of the house to whisper to me.* They *think he cannot talk, but I know better. He told me. He told me everything. He loves me. I held him in my arms all night long, until Maria found us and took him away. I have reached the furthest edge of absurdity. Nothing I do has meaning. They tell me I am mad, and perhaps they are right. I write in my book. I write I could simply take to the air and escape over the tallest cypress, over the beech trees. The soft. Warm. Furry trees.*

From here the journal fell into Italian, and the broken syntax defeated Rachel's understanding. She called the waiter, and paid her bill. Then she walked slowly through the heat towards her hotel.

*   *   *

192

At the desk she found a note from Joshua, which she opened with stiff fingers and a mind numbed by what she had read. Remotely, she made out that he was inviting her to dinner. The time clashed with her arrangement to meet Cellini. A straight choice. She shook her head. He left her a telephone number (which she already had) and asked her to call. *'Please* come. There's a *reason,'* he wrote at the end, and underlined the word twice, as if he feared refusal. But how could she telephone when she was breaking her promise? She thought of him a little guiltily sitting on the Cellini papers. Had he read the others? Were they later journals or poems?

*   *   *

In her room she lay down on her bed and tried to get a grip on her thoughts, which scattered in many directions. Poor child, she thought; poor desperate mother. But something else nagged at her. Another pattern not yet clear but waiting to be fished out of the stream of her inner world. A figure that made sense of Emanuel's hints, and Cellini's minions.

CHAPTER TEN

Rachel's adrenalin was running so high there seemed little point in trying to take a siesta. Instead, she threw off all her clothes, bathed, scrubbed her face, washed her hair and then lay in the bath with her mind racing. Relax, she told herself, while remaining furiously alert. Why was it of any concern to Cellini what had happened so many years ago? Would an old scandal lead him to set his hoods to follow her or break into her room? And she had no doubt that it was his men who had been so responsible. What was there in his *present* life that such a scandal put at risk?

*　　　*　　　*

'You really shouldn't have the water so hot,' her mother's voice whispered from her childhood. 'You'll fall asleep in the bath and drown.'

Poor mother, she remembered suddenly. She had come to say goodbye to her and kissed her hair, saying, 'Everyone has to find a shape for their own life, darling.'

Had her own voice really replied so coldly: 'Why should I care what shape you find?'

She roused herself from the memory. She had not, she admitted to herself, been an especially affectionate daughter.

*   *   *

Giorgio Cellini's white Mercedes was waiting downstairs at exactly 6pm. A gracious dark-skinned chauffeur held open the door, and she climbed into its chilly interior as if in a dream. It was rather like being taken along to be initiated into ritual mysteries, like the woman in *The Story of O*. Or else, she reflected ruefully, like an over-confident Grace Kelly heroine in a Hitchcock film. Probably, if she were in the audience, every nerve would be shrieking an exasperated warning. As Joshua and Ingrid already had, of course. But whatever the journal hinted about his business activities, nothing suggested Cellini was a homicidal maniac. What was there to be afraid of?

*   *   *

Rome is small for a capital city and Rachel was so preoccupied with these thoughts that she did not for a time observe that the car had moved into the suburbs, then taken a southern motorway. When she did, she felt a moment of trapped panic and knocked vehemently on the glass that separated her from the driver.

'*Where* are we going?' she asked, a little rudely.

195

He nodded reassuringly.

'No problem, Signora. I know very well the way.'

'But *yes,*' she cried. 'Si. *E problema per me. Bisognami sapere dove.*'

To which he replied in rapid Italian that she was being taken to Cellini's country house. Giorgio had made no mention of where they were to dine, she recalled. Just as he had taken her acceptance of his invitation for granted.

* * *

Forty minutes later, the car paused in a village with very few houses. The chauffeur turned between two buildings that looked like barns and behind them she made out a pair of wrought iron gates, with heraldic creatures painted in black, gilt and red. For a moment she could not think why they seemed familiar. Then, with a little shock, she recalled that two such gates had been described in Emanuel Cellini's novel. The car entered under an arch in the house wall, into a courtyard, and stopped. The house was much larger than she had guessed from the other side of the archway, and was much older. A servant stepped smartly from the front steps to welcome her.

* * *

It was the family house of an old aristocratic family; perhaps Cellini had bought it, perhaps it had once belonged to his first wife. One room led into another on the ground floor; each very different in décor, with painted ceilings and frescoed walls. In each, and arranged for use rather than for display, was furniture from a later period, probably French: chairs covered in pastel silks, inlaid tables, figurines of Dresden china, delicate Chinese bowls.

* * *

At the far end of the sequence she was led into a room walled in dark green silk, with a wide open window leading to a garden. It was here that Giorgio Cellini awaited her. He sat at the far end of a table, silently, as she approached, one strand of black straight hair falling over his cheek. There was grey in his hair, she observed in the sunlight, but that gave no sense of diminished power. He still looked huge, but for the moment he seemed gentle. Then he rose and came courteously towards her.

'So glad you decided to come,' he said. 'I was afraid my reputation would frighten you away.'

You might have mentioned I was being brought out of Rome,' she said, but there was no anger in her voice. She could feel herself smiling with pleasure: the house was so lovely, the scents from the garden flowers so alluring. And Cellini, here on his own territory, looked less like a villain and more like a man who enjoyed a good day's fishing or a ride over long green fields.

'Don't worry. I will see you get back to your hotel safely. Would you like to look round before we eat?'

She nodded.

'Where shall we begin? This is my favourite room because the ceilings are not too high, and it opens onto the garden. In winter I live on this side of the house too, because it's easier to heat.'

* * *

She found her eyes much taken by a painting of a naked boy, his thighs apart, his penis not so much concealed by a dark red velvety flower as resting upon it. She recognised the face of the boy: it was the same face that had turned round in a smile from his embrace of a goat.

'Can that be a Caravaggio?' she asked cautiously.

'It is said to be. I bought it two years ago. Now he is so fashionable, dealers discover more paintings of course, and perhaps fakers paint more too. I am not a connoisseur.'

'But you have wonderful paintings

everywhere.'

'Those were in the family. My wife's family, I mean. My first wife. I grew up an orphan on the streets of Rome. Would you like to see some of the garden?'

She nodded.

*   *   *

There were banks of jasmine on each side of the path and, at the head of the steps, a statue of three interlinked figures: a lion, a dog and a snake, locked in combat, the lion trying to swallow the dog, the snake coiled round the lion's leg. In the grass beyond, some purple flowers she could not name were beginning to drop their trumpets. A huge bee still found them attractive. As she watched, the furry creature entered one of the trumpets, and then fell with the flower as the trumpet dropped. It was so odd a sight that for the moment she doubted what she had seen, but, as she watched, the bee began a similar assault on another purple trumpet, and the fall was repeated.

*   *   *

She pointed the insect out to Cellini.

'An error in evolution?' she wondered. 'How did such an obsession *survive*?'

'Just as human beings pursue love,' he said,

199

smiling.

He had brought her to a circle of ruined walls.

'The Ancient Romans built here first,' he said. 'Since then there have been infinite numbers of hands constructing, destroying, rebuilding. This house once belonged to a family whose main income came from piracy. One of their sons became a cardinal and built that small chapel dedicated to the Madonna you can see through the trees.'

She shivered.

'Such an enormous house.'

'Yes. It takes a small army of servants to keep the place going.'

'And a small fortune?'

He smiled.

'Not so small. Let us go in again.'

He took her arm firmly to guide her.

'You must wonder why I've asked you here.'

'Yes,' she said.

He paused to point out the blues and golds in Perugino's *Handing Over the Keys to St Peter*.

'This is only a copy,' he said. 'The original is in the Vatican. Now, if we walk through the original dining room, which was badly burned a few years ago, we can get to the terrace. We can talk as we eat.' His voice was disarmingly straightforward. 'I thought I would give you the chance to know another side to the story.'

*   *   *

The table was set with a white cloth; the food under silver hoods to protect it from the midges.

'Sit here,' he suggested, helping her into a chair.

'Why *should* you bother to tell me anything?' she asked.

'You have come at the right moment,' he smiled. 'Do you know we have the first decent government in Italy for years? I have the honour to be part of it. We are going to rebuild Rome, give the ordinary people a chance. Make politics an honest profession again.'

'And you don't want any more newspaper gossip.'

He laughed, a little bitterly.

'Scandal has followed me for thirty years. I have made a practice of saying *nothing* in reply. Many times I could have taken journalists to court, but I never did. Now I think perhaps the time has come to talk.'

'But why to *me*?'

'Because you are a beautiful woman, and I trust your face,' he said. 'Please. Help yourself to the food, and let us begin.'

I don't believe a word of it, she thought.

*   *   *

She took some cold fish, salad and the fried flowers she had eaten last with Doug.

'I know so little,' she said.

He talked as he ate, forking the food into his mouth between sentences, needing no questions.

'About the Mafia first. No one in Sicily is unconnected to the Mafia. It has many arms and it means many different things. Well, I have played a part in its changes. The worst of it is not destroyed. But some people are in gaol. The rule of silence is broken more often than not when we need evidence. It will be a long struggle.'

'I saw in this morning's paper,' Rachel remembered. 'The ones who bombed that judge?'

'Yes. That is a start. There I have been successful. But my own life has not been a happy one.'

'I know,' she said.

'You have seen my son,' he nodded.

'So you had me followed?'

'Of course. And you have read his novel, in any case. So you take everything I say with a pinch of salt. Isn't that the English expression? You are sure I behave like the bastard in his novel?'

'I wouldn't say that,' she said, and remembered the journal she must not mention.

He struck the table.

'Yes. A thug in my own house. A bully to a sick wife. A tyrant to my only son. Can you imagine what it is like to read a book in which you appear as such a figure?'

His indignation was entirely credible, and she murmured some words of sympathy and encouragement.

'Don't pretend. You believe it, like the others.'

He beckoned a servant, who stood in the shadows, and their wine glasses were refilled. She temporized.

'How did you first read the novel?' she asked. 'Did Emanuel give you a copy?'

'Of course not. He wouldn't have dared,' said Giorgio contemptuously. 'No. I read about it for the first time in the press. Think of that. Naturally, I telephoned the head of the publishing house to come and see me.'

'And what did he say?'

'He wouldn't come,' he said, flatly. 'He said the book was already too successful to be negotiable. He would even be *happy* if I sued.'

'Brave of him,' she said.

Well, it is not a small firm, and the man who owns it lives in Miami. But I see what you mean by *brave*. You think I could easily send a few hoods over there? A fantasy.'

'I've no idea how far—'

'Or you think I would if I could, which is as bad. I suppose I have only myself to blame for that. For letting the lies pass without action. But I thought: a novel, after all, how can that hurt me? Books come and go. The pages go brown and rot in libraries. Soon no one will read any of them. Let Emanuel have his little success. It will pass.'

That seems very sensible,' said Rachel.

'No. It was complete shit.'

She swallowed.

'You said you would give me your side of the story.'

'Yes. Look at her. She is very lovely, isn't she?'

He nodded at the wall behind Rachel. Rachel turned her head and recognised the white-faced woman in the painting behind her. The only difference from the sepia photograph was that her eyes were a cobalt blue.

'Yet our marriage was in difficulties from the beginning.'

'Why was that?' asked Rachel.

*   *   *

She put down her glass and resolved to drink no more. She was afraid of giving away something she could only have learnt from the journal. Indeed, she realised the journal had begun to elide with the novel in her mind, almost as if they were by the same hand.

'Some of it was my fault. I admit that. I am rough, I have many uncouth habits. She was too cool and graceful for me. I knew that from the beginning.'

'Why did you marry her?'

'I met her father first. Of course he did not approve of me. But he wanted to go on living in the house of his ancestors. His wife was a younger daughter, without a dowry. Both of them had expensive tastes.'

'I see,' said Rachel. 'So you made a *deal*.'

'She was young and beautiful. I was proud to take her on my arm to expensive occasions.'

'She helped your career?'

'Naturally.' He was impatient now. 'That was part of it. And also she gave me a son. So I did not regret it, although—'

'But what about her? If that counts!' Rachel failed to keep her indignation out of her voice.

'I think she was happy for a time. But she was also a very strange woman, Rachel. She took no pleasure in being a wife and mother. She had no interest in my ambitions.'

'That seems very sad,' said Rachel.

As he glanced up at her, she knew he had heard the false note in her voice.

'I would have been happy to have her enjoy the costliest salon in Rome as a hostess. Would have encouraged it, even. But it wasn't what she wanted.'

'And what was that?' asked Rachel more cautiously.

'She spent hours alone in her room. She was not strong. Having a child had made her ill. There are women who find it very difficult. The doctors agreed with me that the solitude was bad for her health. And she had no time

205

for the boy.'

As he said that, she knew with complete certainty for the first time that he was lying.

'So, what did you do?'

'I tried to help,' he said. 'No more. But you must understand—' He was sharp, and when he paused to study her face she felt her heart beginning to race. 'As a man—I found it difficult. I suppose you care about books.'

'Yes, I do.'

'But you don't make them your whole life. I can see that in the way you move, the way you hold your head.'

'I suppose not.'

'She could. She did. She withdrew into her own world. Long before I behaved badly.'

'How did you behave badly?'

'The usual ways. Powerful men have strong sexual appetites,' he went on. 'Sometimes they have courtesans to minister to them. It's commonplace.'

'Did you expect her to countenance all that?' Rachel shook her head.

'People do. The ruling classes have understood for centuries. But in her case—' He hesitated. 'It shames me to say this. It is a confession. She didn't want me. Not in that way.'

For a moment she was embarrassed to be listening to such an intimate declaration. She bit her lip, then plucked up her courage. She fought to keep what she had learned from the journal out of her voice as she asked the question.

'How did she come to die so young?'

'We found her in the garden. She had jumped from the terrace.'

'How did that happen, do you think?'

'The doctors always said it was likely. She was a clinical depressive. They had suggested shock therapy. Much earlier. I blame myself, but I could not bear the idea. And then, when one of my men saw a chance to make some money by trying to kidnap Emanuel, it tipped her over the edge of sanity. The doctors could do nothing for her. She had to be sedated, to be watched. Perhaps I did not do enough . . .'

'Maybe if you had encouraged her in what she really *cared* about,' began Rachel.

'What do you mean exactly?'

'It might have been a kind of therapy,' she went on, blundering now, she could tell.

He was staring at her. Then he dismissed the man who had been setting out the coffee.

'That's enough. Go to bed,' he told him brusquely.

'Now.' He turned to her again. 'No one will disturb us. What did you have in mind?'

She thought back frantically to the novel, to *anything* other than the journal.

'You described her passion for books. And Emanuel said—' she began.

He seized her wrist.

'Did he give you any of her papers?'

'No.'

She was alarmed by his ferocity, ~~by the~~ speed with which the servant had (scuttled) away, leaving them alone. The beauty of the night had changed its quality. The moon behind the huge cedar tree and the solidity of the flattened branches resembled a toy stage set.

'*Nothing?* Are you sure?'

'Why do you ask?'

Rachel kept her face open, her expression bland.

'Because Emanuel was always fascinated by her scribbling. Of course. He hardly knew her; it was the only way he had to get close to her.'

'Scribbling?'

'Yes. She left him her papers.'

Rachel said nothing, as if she saw no particular significance in that.

'You must wonder why I never read them,' he said. 'Sometimes I wonder why not myself, in all the years after her death when they lay in my possession.'

'You weren't curious?'

'Not then. When you come to write your piece, remember . . .' His voice trailed away. 'Remember it is not easy to be haunted by someone else's unhappiness.'

*   *   *

He dropped her wrist, and she stared down at

the marks left by his fingers.

'I'm sorry,' he said. 'Forgive me.'

She rubbed her arm, and said brightly, 'It's nothing.'

But she was preparing to lift herself out of her chair when the moment presented itself. To escape from him.

'I mean it,' he said roughly. 'I don't *want* you to think badly of me. I brought you here to explain . . .'

'And I promise I understand everything you've told me. You've been very generous with your time. All the same, I think I must go now. It has all been—'

'What did you mean when you spoke of allowing my wife to do what she really *wanted*?'

'In general terms . . . I only meant . . .'

'You spoke of therapy. It *was* therapy, you said, wasn't it? I just want to understand. To have what you said absolutely *clear*.'

'I thought everyone understood what the word "therapy" meant.'

'Psychotherapy?'

'And hobbies. Exercise. All the things people do.'

He had seized her wrist again, and this time, though she let out a cry of pain, he did not release her.

'What *kind* of hobby did you have in mind exactly?'

'Any kind. *Every* kind,' she said, a little

209

shakily. 'How can it make any difference?'

'Let's try this again,' he said carefully. 'You went to my son's flat?'

'Yes.'

'I have never been there. Does he keep it tidily?'

'Very.'

'As a journalist, you will have taken careful note. Describe it to me.'

'It is very plainly furnished. No paintings. No colour.'

'And his study? What did he show you in his study?'

'Not a great deal. Books. Only a computer. No papers at all.'

'No papers. Have I understood that correctly? Did you say there were none at all?'

'Hardly any, then.'

She was sorry she had been so definite, and had answered too quickly.

'Nothing that you carried off to your hotel, for instance?'

He released his grip a little, but she was frightened now, wondering if someone had seen her return, or suspected her trip to Joshua. He must have spies in the Hilton, too. Had anything happened to Joshua? She tried to keep these thoughts out of her face. She had once been an actress. She willed her muscles to keep a puzzled expression. She looked at her watch. It was past midnight.

'I think you had better let me go back to

Rome,' she said steadily.

*   *   *

He let go of her arm, making no attempt to apologise for his casual brutality this time just as she now refused to conceal her dislike of him.

'I hope your chauffeur is not yet in bed. It's very late.'

Perhaps he believed her. She was not sure, and equally unsure why her answers had mattered to him. Her obstinacy sprang only from her promise to Emanuel.

He took her hands again, but gently this time.

'I've had them make up a bed for you.'

'I have to be back in Rome tomorrow.'

'That won't be a problem,' he said.

In reality, she knew she had no choice. She tried to put a bold face on it, and even to smile, though by then she hated his bullying insistence too much even to be afraid of him.

*   *   *

On the way upstairs she refused his arm and walked firmly up the staircase alone. On the landing, as he turned her towards him, she dodged even the formal kiss on her cheek. She was furious at his interrogation. When he showed her to her room, she said a cool goodnight and shut the door quickly behind her.

* * *

It was a white room, like that of a princess in a fairy tale: lace, ruffles, little gilt hanging angels; a ceiling painted in the lightest of pastel pinks and blues. And across the bed lay the sheerest of chiffon nightgowns. What an austere life I have come to lead, she thought, to be pleased by such frivolity. Yet something worried her, even in the pleasure at so much prettiness. It was the familiarity of the room. Cellini had given her a room which she recognised from Emanuel's novel. Rachel made herself go to the curtains and throw them back. There was a French window. A balcony, too, just as she had known there would be. And the shadows of the garden. Night sounds, leaves rustling, and the overpowering sweet perfume of night flowers.

* * *

Things had been kept much as they would have been, she supposed, when Emanuel's unhappy mother lay secluded in this room. There were gilded putti at each corner and a charming, eighteenth century Florentine desk, with cut glass inkpots; the drawers were beautifully made, and spoke to her of another

212

age, when novels were written with pens, and pages blotted with special paper. Each corner of the maroon leather folder that now held the thick vellum was tooled with a ducal coronet. There were still words in mirror writing she could make out: *cuore*, and, less certainly, *Giorgio*.

*   *   *

The bed was made up with fresh sheets. She wondered how many guests Cellini entertained, and whether the room was kept fresh and ready for a visitor any night of the week. There was no harm, she told herself, in sleeping in a room once occupied by Cellini's first wife. In a house this size it would have made no sense to keep all the rooms as aired and fresh as this was. Yet it troubled her.

*   *   *

Rachel could hear the buzz of a mosquito, and knew she should put out the central light and shut the windows. She had to summon some willpower to do so. Staring out across the gardens, she saw how large they were, and how far away she was from the garden wall at the back of the house. No one could hear me if I screamed here, she thought.

*   *   *

Yet why should she scream? Taking herself firmly in hand, she investigated the painted door to see what lay behind the rococo curlicues. Inside, there was a sudden scuffling and when she found the light switch she saw a small green lizard making its escape under the legs of a tall white bath. Its brass legs and taps, the bidet, and the lavatory were as modern and serviceable as that in her hotel. The vaulted ceiling, painted to represent a mountain with a castle on it and a group of figures, was the only oddity.

*   *   *

Looking up at the fresco, which made a semicircle on the domed ceiling, she made out the stretched arms of God the Father and two other figures, both in brightly coloured robes. Another in white—Christ, she conjectured—was placed at one edge, near a few leafless branches of a tree. She supposed the painting represented the story of the withered fig tree, and tried to remember which apostle had attributed that story to Jesus. It was a story she had always disliked—as if it were not punishment enough to be unable to bear fruit, without being blasted for it. It was the gardener or the wasps responsible for fertilisation that should have been blasted, not the tree. As a metaphor, the cruelty was

214

blistering.

*   *   *

Once out of the bathroom, she took a little notebook from her handbag and sat down at the curving, green desk to describe what she had seen. She would have her three thousand words, no problem, if she got back to England alive. The proviso was the thought of a more timorous soul than her own. Why should she fear that she might not? She made out a rumble of thunder, and for a moment the light in the room flickered, but it was a common enough occurrence in country wiring for her to take no particular notice. She was troubled, though, by a claustrophobic sense of imprisonment.

*   *   *

She admired the chiffon nightdress, but could not bring herself to put it on. It seemed too redolent of a lost presence, almost as if it contained a ghost. Not that she believed in ghosts. If the dead have any power, she thought, I have my own dead to protect me.

*   *   *

Unbidden, her father's presence came so physically to her thoughts that it touched her

215

almost to tears. It was as if in this town he once loved, and whose poets he had shared with her as a child, she could remember him again as she had known him in her adolescence. She remembered his smoky jackets, his rough unshaven cheeks, his warm laugh, his generosity. No wonder she thought of her father in Rome. It was his city. He had made it his own, as London had never been, nor the Dublin of his childhood either. She let herself wonder about him, how he had kept himself so free of bitterness, whether he regretted his brief foray into the world of English high society. Sometimes it seemed as if he had been the only man who had ever loved her generously, despite all the others who had implored her to let them enter her bed. Certainly Christopher had never put himself out to protect her. And she refused to think of the others, even though they came in a line of supplicants across her memory as she lay back on the pillows.

*　　　*　　　*

She brought herself to turn the brass switch on the bedside lamp, and settled to sleep. Just behind the cedar tree sat a huge moon, fading a little at one side but filling the room with its light nonetheless. She could hear the wood move in the floor as the temperature changed, as it had once moved in old houses of her childhood. But she was nowhere near drifting off to sleep, for all the hot bath. It will be morning soon, and I can leave, she told herself. And with that thought, the tension began to relax in her limbs and she fell into a short dream. She was running away from soldiers, perhaps Germans; running away along corridors of rooms with her white nightdress streaming behind her. Somewhere in a Roman street, against a wall pocked with bullets, stood a man in a trilby hat who looked like her father. He was on his own, smoking, his expression hidden. There was a shot. And, when she saw him fall, she turned hysterically on the soldiers.

'You bastards, you bastards!' she screamed. 'He had done nothing. Why? Help him. *Help.*'

And then she was awake and there was a knocking on her door.

*   *   *

At first she thought she was imagining the knocking, that she had invented the noise in her terror, that it was part of her dream. It stopped as she sat up in bed, but then it began again. It was an unignorable human hand, not a creak of wood or a figment of her imagination.

I'll just lie here, she thought. Until whoever it is goes away.

Then the handle turned and, in the light of

the corridor, she saw Cellini.

'Are you all right? You screamed,' he said.

'It was only a nightmare,' she said, far from reassured to see him and to make out that he slept naked.

'Are you sure?' He approached the bed and looked down at her. 'I should not have put you in here.'

'Yes. *Why* did you?' she asked.

Rachel was sitting upright in the bed, the lacy white sheets clutched to her throat in a gesture which felt less modest than defensive.

'I'm sorry. People *do* sleep badly here. There are so many other rooms. I should have been more considerate, but you seemed so matter-of-fact.'

'I don't believe in ghosts,' she said, 'if that's what you mean. Do you?'

He sat on the bed without apology.

'There are many kinds of ghosts,' he said. 'My wife's ghost walks the world with the help of my son. She undoes every work I try to bring to completion. May I stay for a while?'

Any comfort she had taken from his human presence disappeared in a quite different anxiety.

'I would much rather you went back to your room.'

'Please,' he said. 'You can help me.'

'Why should I help *you*? Why do you need help?'

'A haunted man pursued by a ghost? A silly

question. There is a resemblance. I saw it at once.'

'To the lady in the painting?'

'Yes. Perhaps you are a relation?'

'It is a very characteristic English face. She resembled my mother more than me,' said Rachel reluctantly, wanting to distance herself from what he was saying.

'These things must be exorcised. Any way that they can.'

'I don't think so,' she said. 'I have no responsibility to do anything of the kind.'

'Yes. Don't you see? And you *want* to—'

'I certainly *don't*,' said Rachel.

He did not bother to argue. Instead he took her naked body into his arms and kissed her. She felt his strong, thick tongue in her mouth. He was hurting her: the hand gripping her shoulder was ferocious; she could feel the flesh under it bruising, even as his mouth on hers stilled her cry of pain. Then she was lying across the bed, and one thumb and finger were rubbing and sliding into her. To her shame afterwards, her bare legs adjusted themselves so he could thrust into a body which was no longer unwilling.

*   *   *

When his body stopped moving, she could see through the window a single glowing star, so blue and bright she wondered if it was a

219

planet. His body remained in hers and pleasure returned to her in wave after wave even as she watched the single glow in the blackness.

* * *

In the morning, she woke to the sound of rolling thunder; a storm had broken in the night. She was alone in the bed. She was not surprised, and not entirely sure the encounter with Cellini had not been a dream. In the sunlight the room looked shabbier. Through the window she could see the rain splashing on the grey stone of the balcony and, beyond, a cloud hung in the cypress trees. She could see now that there were olives and vineyards beyond the formal garden. What had seemed so persuasive in his presence was less so in his absence. This morning there was even a certain vulgarity in the perfect trim of the curtains, the lace on the pillows, the gilt furniture. But she was glad to have woken early: she wanted to get back to Rome.

* * *

She showered and dressed thoughtfully, without alarm but a little disgusted at the pleasure she had taken the night before. It had been such a brutal sensuality, void of the least exchange of human feeling. Even as she

220

recalled as much, a little echo of the intense pleasure she had experienced ran through her body. So Joshua was right, she thought miserably. She had learnt less about Cellini than she had learnt about herself.

*   *   *

When she came back from the bathroom there was a breakfast tray, fresh coffee and a note written on an envelope which assured her the car was at her disposal to take her back to her hotel. Then she noticed the envelope was not empty and shook the contents onto the table. Even as she made out the rattle of metal on wood, her heart clenched: the metal was a gold bracelet: a thick, gold woven band, of the kind she had noticed in expensive shops on the Via Condotti. It was not that she wanted any continuation of the relationship. Well, there had been no relationship. But she was disappointed in the crudity of his response. Their encounter had been a transaction like any other; no doubt geared to her special needs, but otherwise unremarkable. She was paid and dismissed. Even though she suspected the gold bracelet might be worth as much as the fee from the *Sunday Enquirer*, she let it fall on the breakfast tray without hesitation.

*   *   *

221

As she travelled back into Rome, she was still angry with herself. She felt cheap and a little stupid. She pulled herself together only when the car reached the outskirts of the city. Now she must write an article in the hotel and have it ready to type and fax to Ridley Martin from her home computer.

*　　*　　*

Reaching her hotel room, she switched on the reassuring, bland voice of CNN. Except there was nothing bland about what she then heard: that a group of English journalists had been taken prisoner in Sumatra.

CHAPTER ELEVEN

'Sumatra still uses water power,' said the newscaster. 'It's a very primitive economy.' The screen showed a group of young women using stones to grind corn. 'There are still tigers in the jungle.'

'Yes, yes!' Rachel wanted to scream impatiently at the handsome, well-cut face. 'But what's happening *now*?'

'Now we're going over to Charles Edwards. a former US diplomat in the Far East,' said the same bland voice, and an ageing Senator smiled from a side screen reassuringly. He looked calm, well-fed and very happy to be sitting in his armchair in Washington.

*   *   *

'These are worrying developments,' he said, with great solemnity. "There's clearly been a crackdown by the new government. In Jakarta, several local journalists have been harassed and assaulted. Two have been taken to hospital. The local media have begun to compare the Democratic People's Party to the banned Communist Party, which is particularly ominous if you remember what happened when that party was declared illegal a few years back. Naturally, the US government and *all* civilised governments will be watching these developments with deep concern.'

*   *   *

'And the Sumatra incident?' the interviewer asked.

There was a pause.

'I have no information about that.'

'Is it, in your view, *connected* to the upheaval in Jakarta?'

'The Indonesian government may well be preparing the ground for massive new repression all over their vast country.'

'Do we know which Americans have been

taken prisoner?'

'We don't have many details about the youngsters. Only one is American; we think he is a student. The other may be a British travel journalist.'

'Is it possible that either of them is a threat to the stability of the region?'

'Most unlikely.'

'No CIA involvement?'

'Absolutely not,' said the diplomat curtly.

*   *   *

Rachel's mouth was dry. She could not swallow. Her body was clenched on the bed, her hands were fists; the nails bit into her palms. What to do? What to do? Who could help? *Indonesia.* She knew nothing about the country, though she had watched the riots, and the departure of the president.

*   *   *

I'll have to fly there. If I can. If they'll let me. I'll have to do something. The gaolers must want something. Some ransom, perhaps. I'll get it. Beg it. When she thought of Tom's beauty and courage and how little his wish to make his own way would mean to the captors who held him, tears stung her eyes, though she brushed them away furiously. She would have liked to bargain with God. To pray. It was a very long while since she had experienced that wish.

*　　　*　　　*

Her body was still frozen into a stasis of misery when the telephone rang. She picked it up at once with a snatch of hope. Perhaps help was already on its way. Or at least news. It might be the English Ambassador.

*　　　*　　　*

Instead it was Christopher, and his voice— even more clipped and English now he was back in Australia—had an edge of reproach in it.

'At last! I've been trying to find you for hours. It hasn't been easy.'

'Never mind that,' she said impatiently.

'Well, thank you very much.'

'I mean, it isn't *relevant* is it, at the moment? I'm glad you found me. Is there any news?'

'I've been in touch with the Foreign Office,' he said. 'They'll keep us informed. Try not to get hysterical.'

And at that, she did burst into tears; a wild and helpless sobbing that he listened to for only a short time before breaking in:

'This won't help Tom. But I don't suppose that's the point. Cry if you have to.'

'It doesn't matter about me,' she said, when

225

she could speak. 'It doesn't matter about me in the *least*. All I *care* about, all I've *ever* cared about, all my whole life has been . . .' And then her sobs began uncontrollably again.

'Then you should have stopped Tom going off on this foolhardy trip,' said Christopher, with sudden heat. 'Don't you *read* the newspapers? Was a bit of money and cheap fame worth risking Tom's life for? You should never have let him go. If you want to weep, weep for your own stupidity. Or maybe your neglect. Whichever.'

His words would once have hurt her; she would have thought it was his intention to do so. In her present state, she barely registered what he was saying, and the rest of the conversation went by without her even trying to enter it. It was all so trivial beside the anguish of Tom frightened, captive and alone.

*   *   *

After she had put the receiver back in its cradle, she pondered for a moment what remained of *anything* that had seemed interesting to her before the CNN news flash. It was all of no account whatsoever. All her worrying about what had she done with her life, and her wretched talent. What did any of that matter now? This fantasy she had of earning a few extra thousand, how could that signify if there were no Tom to benefit?

How frivolous now seemed all the other concerns of her life. How shallow she had become, she reflected. For what had she worked so hard the last few days—the chance of money, a sexual thrill? When all the time she cared about nothing but Tom. No one else matters, she thought. He's all there is. And, since she had not realised how central a place he occupied in her emotional landscape, how could Tom have known it? She had been so worried not to cumber him with her need, perhaps he had hardly guessed it was there. Perhaps now he would never know.

*   *   *

Even to think of a world with such a blankness was so alarming that for a moment it was all she could do to hold on to consciousness. It was like a road accident. There was *before*, and there was *after*, and no survivor was exactly the same person.

*   *   *

Please God, she began. Please God. He's not yet twenty. How can you be so unfair? And then she had to berate herself for the naïveté. As if the random suffering of other people was something she had never taken on board. As if she had known of that unfairness only at a distance up till now, and never felt it in her own body. So *often* Tom had known how to help her, and now there was no way she could help him.

$$* \qquad * \qquad *$$

Please God, she said. Please listen to me.

$$* \qquad * \qquad *$$

It was the same God who had not listened to Frank O'Malley, who had not let him cheat the statistical curve for all his endurance, the God who had let a million young children go into the ovens. Why should he be listening to Rachel O'Malley?

$$* \qquad * \qquad *$$

Please God, she nevertheless said out loud. *Let them not be hurting him.*

$$* \qquad * \qquad *$$

She'd watched so proudly as Tom packed his suitcase for this trip. He was so jaunty about the expenses paid, and the cheque at the other end, and confident that he knew what he wanted to do with his life. Could everything suddenly be taken away from him?

$$* \qquad * \qquad *$$

Of course it could. At Frank O'Malley's funeral, friends spoke of his courage and dignity in the face of the cancer that had eaten him with such rapidity. There were women crying whom Rachel did not know, and her mother, ashen-pale, on the arm of an old friend. Everyone loved him. How could God not have loved him? Silly question, false premise.

*　　*　　*

And then she remembered Joshua. He was not the most obvious person to have information; it was doubtful if his name would carry much weight among the Sumatra military, but she could talk to him. It would help to talk to him. He would at least know what she was feeling.

*　　*　　*

She rang the Hilton, and there was an interminable pause while the hotel tried his room—evidence at least that he had not checked out—and then, at her pleading, paged him in the bar.

*　　*　　*

When at last he came to the phone, he sounded a little disgruntled, and she

229

remembered her sulky refusal to phone after his last note.

'To what am I indebted?' he drawled, on hearing her voice.

'Listen,' she pleaded. 'This is an emergency. What do you know about Sumatra?'

'I was there for a week or two in 1993,' he said. 'Lovely place. Unspoiled white beaches. Miles of palm trees.'

'I'm not asking for a brochure. Just a minute. Hold on, will you?'

The news had come round again. She listened as the same interview was repeated and then silenced the Senator with a flick of the remote control.

'Hello, hello? Joshua?'

'I haven't rung off,' he said. 'Though a lot of people would. Do I take it you are talking to me while listening to the television?'

'You don't understand. It's Tom. My son Tom,' she began. 'I just heard on CNN. He's been taken prisoner in Indonesia. I don't know what to do. What *can* I do?'

'I'll call you back when I've found out what's going on,' he said.

*   *   *

There followed an acre of time which the watch on her wrist claimed took up no more than two and a half minutes. In that space, she imagined Tom's slight body on a mud floor, heard the clang of thick metal doors, saw boots, truncheons, arms, cries of pain. Tried to put out of her mind the thought of guns. Mistakes. His life at the whim of some uncomprehending adolescent, some accident of politics, some mistaken order.

*   *   *

When the telephone went, she expected Joshua, but instead it was Ingrid Donkins.

'I can't talk now,' said Rachel.

'I thought you'd like to know,' Ingrid began nevertheless, 'that poor Beatrice is very upset.'

'I don't give a fuck,' said Rachel. 'I can't talk *now*. Please get off the line, could you!'

Ingrid gave a startled grunt. She wasn't used to rudeness from Rachel.

'Is something wrong?'

'Yes,' said Rachel. 'Something is bloody awful. It's Tom. He's in gaol in Sumatra.' Then she rang off, before Ingrid could offer condolences or say anything about star signs.

*   *   *

Did she perhaps say she'd meet Joshua in the lobby? She wasn't sure. Time had now altogether stopped moving, she thought miserably. I've looked at this watch four times and the hands have not shifted. If only I could think of something else. Instead, she began

231

remembering Tom as a child. Of his loneliness at school. And her own selfishness, tripping off on one jaunt after another and leaving him with nannies and au pairs. She thought of his self-taught cleverness; the way he talked with such precocity, like many an only child of a single mother; understanding the grown-up world of pain and humour long before he entered it. How fiercely she had felt when he was bullied as a child; the thought of him being bullied now was intolerable. She was drenched, not with the perspiration of heat but the sweat of terror. Crude terror. She opened the mini bar. Took a whisky out. Didn't turn the screw top because she knew it wouldn't help. Nothing would help if anything happened to Tom.

*   *   *

The volume was turned down on the television, but when the news bulletin came up again, she flicked it up. The newsreader had begun to question another red-faced American in a boxed screen on the right of his desk. A line of white type beneath the box identified him as a distinguished Senator in Washington, who had been an ambassador to Indonesia two decades earlier.

'You have to understand the Indonesian authorities are jumpy,' he was saying. 'The United States' policy is not to encourage any

232

of its nationals to enter the scene at the moment. No panic. No crisis. But we are recommending that any tourists make at once for the airports, where European and US flights are standing by to remove them from the area.'

'There are reports that a group of hill guerillas have links to Muslim extremists.'

'I have no such information. There is a great deal of speculation. I don't think it's particularly helpful at this stage.'

'But they are hostages?'

'We don't even know that. As I say, I don't think it is in the interests of the young men concerned to answer such questions at the moment.'

*   *   *

He might be right, but he was hardly a hot line to what was happening now, thought Rachel, as another figure, this time a Professor at the University of Maryland, appeared on the boxed screen.

'The Association of Muslim Intellectuals', he explained, 'believes Sumatra can only be brought into the twenty-first century if the general technology of the West can be brought into Sumatra. Back in 1979, the preachers and scientists who pushed that point of view had to go on the run. They went into hiding because the Indonesian government didn't approve of those ideas. But the present government is moving towards the same position. So this incident is hard to explain. Westerners are no longer seen as devilish, certainly not since the departure of President Soharto, so that . . .'

The drone of his voice was urgently interrupted by the newscaster. Some news was coming in on another line.

*   *   *

There was a photograph of an Englishman now, standing in front of a hotel with a curving roof. The white type underneath said he was speaking from Padang, in south western Sumatra. Rachel's heart lurched wildly as she saw as much, her front teeth pressing into her lower lip.

'The good news,' he was saying, 'is that the hill tribe guerillas who were feared to have captured the two young men have totally denied it. Almost certainly they are not in guerilla hands but in military custody, charged with spying.'

*   *   *

Then the satellite link failed, and whatever he was trying to explain about that situation was inaudible and, as she came close up to the screen to try and read his lips, CNN switched back to the studio and the news switched to

234

the stock exchange in the Far East. When the telephone went, she clutched at the receiver like a friendly hand, hoping it would be Joshua.

*   *   *

Instead she recognised the cool, clipped voice of Sir Peter Forrest, and she pulled herself together to reply as he would expect.

'Rachel? Are you all right? Good girl. Anna wondered if you would like us to come and collect you.'

'I think I'd better stay where I can be found.'

She had indeed barely moved since the news first came in.

'Be sensible. We are in close touch with London here.'

'Even so,' she said.

She wasn't quite sure why it seemed important, but she needed to be where Joshua could reach her when he rang back.

'Look, there won't be a problem about *finding* you,' said Peter. 'I'll arrange for the hotel to transfer any calls over here. You won't miss anything, I promise.'

Then Anna Forrest came on the telephone, her voice natural and familiar.

'Rachel, what a nightmare. You *are* brave.'

'No, I'm not,' said Rachel, suddenly doubting if she could maintain the correct

235

English manner in a long-drawn-out siege of waiting.

'I remember what it was like when one of our sons had to be airlifted out of Bosnia.'

Rachel remembered the incident only remotely.

'He was driving food in, you know, and his jeep crashed. He was flown home by an aeroplane paid for by some little bucket shop insurance firm on the Kilburn High Road.'

Rachel tried to imagine the relief of such an outcome.

'I was *terrified*,' said Anna. 'Don't feel you have to keep a stiff upper lip or anything. Listen, we've gallons of scotch, a huge TV and every channel in the world. There's cold food if you want any, and you don't have to eat if you don't. No sense sitting it out on your own.'

'All right,' said Rachel, weakening.

'Have you heard from Christopher?'

'Yes,' said Rachel.

'He phoned here first. He's out of his mind with worry, you know.'

'Is he?'

'Yes. Angry with *you*, of course.'

'I gathered that.'

'Don't worry. All the calls will be transferred to us. And perhaps Peter can help in some way,' said Anna. 'We'll send the car.'

*　　　*　　　*

The last few days felt like a sick dream to Rachel now. 'What did I think I was *doing*?' she moaned to herself, thinking of her pleasure in Cellini's bed. What kind of story had she hoped to uncover? She should have understood how it was for both those lonely women. With what *cruelty* she had probed into Beatrice's soul, for nothing more than a little money. A *very* little money. Just enough to pay a few pressing bills. And now in her agony of suspense she would have let go of every penny she owned in the world willingly to have nothing worse to face than the usual crop of brown envelopes on the morning mat.

*   *   *

Joshua had still not telephoned when a call came from the lobby that the car was downstairs. By then, whether or not the call came seemed less important. The TV screen had begun to show the prison building where Tom and his American friend were being kept. They said the names. There was no mistake possible.

*   *   *

At the Ambassador's house, Rachel sat between Peter and Anna on a leather chesterfield in front of a huge television screen, watching BBC news. All three held tumblers of scotch. It was Rachel's second tumbler, in fact. As far as she could tell, the alcohol was not reaching her bloodstream; certainly it was having no effect whatsoever.

*   *   *

The last news bulletin from London had not mentioned the incident. The headlines focused on a disturbance in an Irish protest march, something about a rise in mortgage rates, then went into coverage of Wimbledon. Rachel was incredulous.

'That's *good*,' said Peter, reassuringly. 'That means there are negotiations.'

'Negotiations,' she repeated blankly.

'For the boys' release. That must be why the press has been called off.'

'What exactly is happening in Indonesia now Soharto has gone?'

'His regime hasn't gone, of course.'

'Where does Great Britain stand on that? Do we *back* the regime?'

'Well, we wanted to see the PKI out of action in the sixties. Naturally. I don't know if the Foreign Office would like it thought the UK helped to bring Soharto to power,' said Peter dubiously.

'PKI?'

'The Indonesian Communist Party.'

'What is going on *now*? That's what I need to know.'

238

'The situation is pretty volatile. The economy is collapsing. There are separatist movements.'

'And what about Sumatra?'

'Muslim, and quiet for the most part.'

Rachel thought very hard about what he was saying.

'Is the UK involved in *any* of it? Don't we have some preferences?'

'Well, of course we wouldn't want the whole structure splitting apart. Very unstable for the whole region.'

'At the moment, then, who do you imagine we would be negotiating with?'

'Essentially the army, I'd have thought. It could take a little time, though. Perhaps you should try and get some sleep. Would you like to try?'

'I'd rather just sit here, thanks.'

You might drop off, all the same,' he observed, taking the empty glass out of her hand.

* * *

Upright as she was, she must have fallen into some kind of sleep, because she was woken by the sound of a telephone, and Anna, in a billowing apricot nightdress, gently shaking her shoulder. The alcohol Rachel had been drinking made itself felt as she tried to get to her feet.

'You don't need to move,' said Anna, gently urging the cordless phone into her hand.

* * *

It wasn't Joshua, as she had been certain it would be, it was her mother, phoning from Latin America.

'Is it the middle of the night where you are? I'm sorry.'

Rachel looked at her wristwatch.

'Closer to morning.'

Her head was spinning.

'Darling, I can't believe my *eyes*. Is it true? Is it Tom?'

'Yes,' Rachel replied shortly. Her throat was too dry to say more.

'What is happening over there? Can't something be done to get him back? Have you been in touch with the Prime Minister?'

Rachel admitted she had not.

'Well, you must get on the telephone immediately. What are you thinking of? It doesn't matter if you don't know him personally. *I'll* do it if you like.'

'Mother, I'm not sure that would help.'

* * *

Rachel was irritated by the familiar certainties she heard in her mother's voice. At the same time, as she became aware that Anna had flicked up the sound on the television remote control, that irritation became irrelevant. A pulse began racing in her throat, and the blood in her ears drowned out other sounds.

'Is that *Tom* they are bringing out on a stretcher?' asked Anna.

'Yes, it is,' said Rachel, her eyes taking in the image of Tom, pain unmistakable in his face, handcuffed to the bed he was carried on.

*　　　*　　　*

When the camera came up to him, he tried to smile but she could see how much he had been hurt. His wide mouth was pale, his eyes red, his fine hair sweat-drenched and brown. What could he tell them if they pressed him with questions? She could not imagine. He had done nothing. She reminded herself he was clever. But her heart sank. Anyone could be broken. All torturers knew that. What if he confessed to some meaningless political act which would put him outside any Foreign Office help, behind the scenes or not?

*　　　*　　　*

Apparently her mother was watching a similar programme, half the world away. Rachel became aware of a voice babbling from the phone in her hand, and as she lifted the receiver to her ear she could hear the dismay

241

in her mother's voice, though she could barely listen to the words she was saying.

'You *poor* child. I can imagine just how you feel.'

'Can you?'

'You aren't alone, I hope.'

'No. I'm with Anna Forrest.'

'Who?'

Rachel explained, as if to someone on another planet. Her eyes were fixed on the screen as if a blink might lose some important clue to what was going on. Even so, she could make out the pathos and loneliness in her mother's voice. She's an old woman, Rachel realised suddenly. And she loves Tom, too.

*   *   *

Her mother made no comment on her prolonged silence.

'I'll call later,' she was saying. 'I realise I haven't exactly been a devoted mother, but I do care. Tom is my only grandchild, you know.'

'I'm so sorry,' Rachel said into the receiver and to Anna at the same time. The pulse in her throat and the beat of the blood in her ears had increased their pace alarmingly.

'Are you all right?'

'I feel a little faint,' said Rachel.

The image of Tom's pale face still filled her brain, though it had gone from the screen.

'How is your mother?'

'I forgot to ask,' Rachel said slowly.

*　　　*　　　*

A single ebullient bird began to sing outside the open windows, the piercing melody of a new day. As Rachel looked, the light in the windows was already that of early morning.

'Come and have a shower,' Anna said. 'You'll feel better.' Rachel agreed, but could not move.

*　　　*　　　*

Then Peter appeared, in a plaid dressing gown, and said, 'The officer holding the boys is about eighteen. There's an interview with him on CNN.'

*　　　*　　　*

There was no sign of Tom on his stretcher now. For a moment Rachel wondered if she had dreamed the sight of him. He and his friend were presumably in the building behind the palm trees. All that could be seen was a well-dressed officer and a journalist with a microphone, asking questions. What assurance could the Western world have that the captives were being well fed and unharmed? The young officer replied fluently, but not quite

243

comprehensibly, and the subtitles faltered.

'What did he say? For God's sake, what did he say?' cried Rachel.

The journalist stuck to his script, though no doubt equally confused. Would it be possible to come and see the captive with the broken leg? No, it would not. The emphatic shake of the head looked clear enough. Was he receiving medical treatment? Of course.

* * *

All the blood drained from Rachel's head and she experienced a wave of nausea. So, Tom's leg was broken. She wondered what kind of medicine was practised in Indonesia.

'Don't worry,' said Peter, guessing her fears. 'They have analgesics. And antibiotics.'

Rachel excused herself, and went to vomit up everything she had eaten in the last twenty-four hours.

* * *

When she came back, the television had left the story and begun to report a bombing in Atlanta.

'That's a good sign,' said Peter, who had been in touch with the Foreign Office. 'Negotiations are still going on.'

'Any *other* phone calls?' she asked.

'Yes,' said Anna. 'Joshua Silk. He'll phone

244

again.'

*   *   *

When the phone rang almost immediately, however, it was Christopher.

Well, at least you had the sense to leave a phone number with the hotel,' he said. 'Am I getting you out of bed?'

'I haven't been to bed.'

'I haven't slept either. I don't suppose there's anything new, is there? They seemed to have stopped reporting on the situation over here.'

For the first time she believed that he cared what happened as much as she did, and gently repeated Peter's words of reassurance. His response was a groan.

'He would say that. Let's hope it's true.'

There was a silence between them which she could not find the right words to break.

'Think of families holding on for years and years,' he said. 'Just *hoping*.'

His voice was hollow with fatigue and, like her mother, he sounded older.

'Are you all right?' she asked him.

'No, I'm not.' He laughed. 'Funny you should ask. Had a bypass a few months ago, actually. Not too good for me to have so much adrenalin coursing round the system. And my wife won't even let me soothe myself with a bottle of scotch.'

'Alcohol doesn't help,' she said. 'You're lucky to have someone looking after you.' She roused herself to take an interest in his new life. 'How are your children?'

'The girls are fine. Very Australian. Hiking through the outback. They have me written off as a pommie wimp.'

'And life in Sydney?'

'It's okay. What about you? Your health, I mean? It's all that counts at our time of life.'

'I'm fine.'

'No dyspepsia?'

'No.'

'I behaved quite badly at the end, you know, when your father was dying. I do realise that. There was so much else going on for me you didn't even *know* about . . .'

'For God's sake, Christopher, it's not important now. What are you saying?'

'I wondered if, I mean if this all comes out all right, maybe we could finally try—'

His voice trailed off and she was bewildered.

Try *what*? Forgive one another?'

'Yes, I suppose so. Something like that.'

'Nothing's coming out right yet,' said Rachel.

*   *   *

'You really must get some sleep,' said Anna. 'You'll be ill otherwise. There's a bed made up two doors away. And I've put a small television in there, though the story has gone cold now, and Peter says there won't be any news for a bit. Come on.'

Rachel allowed herself to be led away. She was numb with fatigue, which proved a better tranquillizer than alcohol. When she lay on the bed, fully clothed, she was insensible in minutes.

*   *   *

She woke hazily a couple of hours later, with a vague sense that something unspecified was wrong. Then memory returned in a wave of pain all the sharper for the brief respite. Somewhere in her sleep a telephone had been ringing, she guessed, as she leapt from the bed. In the corridor she could hear Anna and Peter talking together in low voices.

'What's happened?' she cried out, conscious that in her unkempt state she must look like a woman crazed.

'There's a call for you. We were wondering whether to wake you.'

She took the cordless phone and sank into a chair. Her hand was shaking and her palms left a wet mark on the receiver. This time it was Joshua.

'I've spoken to Reuters' stringer who used to cover Padang. He's in Malaysia now. He doesn't know much. Most of the journalists

247

left yesterday, but he said there's nothing on the news because they don't want anything to go wrong. So hold on. Stay calm. All right?'

'Don't go,' she said. 'Keep talking. What happened? Why Tom?'

'It was a mistake,' he said. 'A misunderstanding. I'll get back to you.'

His voice seemed to be the only sound in the whole world that had any element of reassurance and contact.

'I *think* he was photographing a parade,' Joshua said, with that rising dubious note in his voice that would once have had her laughing. 'He thought it was colourful, I expect. I'll get back to you in a few minutes.'

'When will it be sorted out? Don't ring off,' she pleaded, her panic rising at the thought of disconnection.

'Be sensible. There's a call coming in on the other line.'

'Can I hold on?' she said.

She could tell he hadn't rung off because she could hear a babble of other voices in the background. There were a great many voices, including Joshua's voice, rising in what might have been alarm. Then he was back on the phone again.

'I'll call you as soon as there's news.'

Reluctantly, she put the receiver back in the cradle.

*　　*　　*

'I think you need to wash and change,' said Anna.

Rachel caught a glimpse of herself, still in the clothes she had been wearing the day before, her hair sticking sweatily from her head like a sick dog.

'We could have someone go and collect your suitcase, if you like. Or you can try on one of my daughter's summer dresses. You seem much of a size. God knows how you do it. Then you'd better have some lunch.'

Rachel pulled herself together with an enormous effort and opted for a summer dress. She did not want her cases taken away from the hotel.

'Your mother phoned again, by the way. I told her you would call when you woke up.'

*   *   *

In the bathroom, Rachel felt a small and qualified hope begin to take shape. Peter's reassurance she had recognised as professional. Almost part of his job. Joshua had no such habit. How did he find the Reuters' man? she wondered.

*   *   *

In a summer dress, with her hair washed and combed, she looked almost normal, apart from her face which was white as a stone. The thought of lunch remained abhorrent to her. She could only eat a few slices of tomato and drink a glass of water. Anna clucked over her like one of her own children.

'*Honestly*, Rachel, I can't see what good it will do if you die of starvation.'

'I know. I ought to eat. It's just impossible,' she tried to explain.

Then she repeated to Peter what Joshua had said.

'Sounds reliable. Good,' said Peter, though less enthusiastically than she would have liked. She made out something new in his voice, as if he had other thoughts he was not revealing. Perhaps it was simply that he disapproved of Joshua Silk.

'Can we have the TV on again?' she asked.

He seemed reluctant to allow her to go to the set, and now she saw clearly in his face that there was another twist to the story.

'What's happened?' she cried.

Peter sounded apologetic.

'There seems to have been another explosion of discontent all over Java. Hardly surprising, in one of the poorest nations in the world. Nothing to do with Tom, of course. Another island, hundreds of miles from Sumatra. Do bear that in mind. There's some rather scary footage, though. Are you sure you want to look?'

'Yes, I want to look,' said Rachel, her chin

firm. Peter turned on the TV and all three stared into the screen with horror. At first Rachel could not make out what she was seeing. Bodies in a ditch, face downwards, seemingly half naked. In her terror she could not at first take in the words of the newsreader and only caught the end of what was being said: 'The civilised world . . . atrocities of this order . . .' It was Indonesia, all right.

Rachel was trembling and violently sick now; she had to run to the bathroom, before coming weakly back to watch again. What had happened to these young men was so unspeakable that the camera was not allowed to close in on their mutilated bodies. But even from the note in the voice of the newscaster she understood: these were not white people. They were local journalists. Indonesian. She was disgusted by the feeling of relief that flooded her as that became clear; as if those poor boys were not the children of mothers as incredulous and tormented as herself.

*   *   *

The afternoon went by in dazed attention, with very little fresh news. Rachel gave her air tickets to Peter, who said he would arrange for an emergency extension. He also suggested that her luggage be brought from the hotel, but Rachel still opposed the idea. She wasn't sure why. From time to time, there were phone calls for Peter. Rachel drank a good deal of English breakfast tea, which seemed to be the only liquid she dared allow to pass her lips.

*   *   *

As the light began to go out of the sky, Rachel faced the possibility of another night without news. At some remote part of her consciousness, she heard Anna and Peter discussing whether she could be left alone in front of the TV while they went to the opening of a civic centre that evening. She tried to explain it wasn't the night she was afraid of; her body ached with the need for sleep. What she was afraid of was waking once again into the knowledge of Tom's danger. And that would be there whether they stayed behind or not.

'Of course you must go,' she told them. 'I'll be fine.'

And since such receptions were an important part of their job, they left her to it. She sat, a small, childlike figure in the huge sitting room, more alone than she had ever felt in her life.

*   *   *

Rachel would have liked to telephone Joshua again for more information. She didn't because she didn't want to block the line. She looked at the silent green telephone. And remembered. How sometimes she had waited of an evening for some man to phone, or Christopher perhaps, at the time he was moving out. And the childish suspense of that waiting now seemed altogether petty. She began to sob helplessly: broken, frightened sobs. Like a child crying, she thought. And hoping for comfort. As if there were anything in the world that could comfort her if Tom were hurt. Or trapped far away, lonely and beyond help. She would not even let herself think of the blackest possibility.

* * *

At seven-thirty a servant came to enquire what she would like for supper. She asked for a sandwich and a beer to be sent to the living room, unable to bear the thought of leaving the television. When the food came, she could eat nothing. She simply sat and waited and watched until the shadows outside her window changed into darkness.

* * *

When the phone finally rang it wasn't Joshua. It was Emanuel Cellini.

'Go away,' she said, and put down the receiver without even wondering what he could possibly want, or why he should so much have overcome his reluctance to engage with anyone in the outside world.

*   *   *

Perhaps he hadn't heard what she said, because he rang back immediately, and his unhappiness was clear in his voice. She made a tremendous effort not to snap at him. He wasn't steely and strong like Ingrid Donkins. He was a frightened boy with a terrible history.

'Please,' she explained. 'I have to keep the line clear. I'm waiting for important news. I'll phone you later.'

'All right,' he said.

*   *   *

As if to reward her self-discipline, the next phone call was, astonishingly, the voice of Tom himself. She would have recognised the tones of it anywhere, even though he sounded shaky. For a moment she was afraid she was dreaming.

'Where are you?' she asked, afraid to hear this miracle was the one phone call allowed from some unspeakable police cell.

'In Padang,' he said. 'I'm okay.'

'Not in prison?'

'In a four star hotel. With a funny upturned roof like all the houses round here, drapes round the bed and a bar for residents only. I'm

254

having a double scotch.'

They didn't hurt you?' she whispered.

'Not very much.'

She caught her breath.

'Well, I've a broken ankle,' he said. 'You'll see when I get back. Don't worry. The medicine here is surprisingly Western.'

'But what *happened*?' she wanted to know.

'It was all a great fuss about nothing. Some academic got us out.'

'A journalist?'

'You must be *joking*, Mother! The foreign press is keeping out of Indonesia for the time being. No. Some local professor.'

'Why did he?'

'I suppose the Foreign Office did some kind of deal. Jim, that's the American, has already gone. He wasn't . . . you know . . . damaged. They're putting me on the next plane.'

*   *   *

And then the line went dead. She didn't understand, but perhaps it didn't matter how he'd been rescued, since he seemed to be so. A broken ankle didn't seem so bad. People did worse things to themselves on the ski slopes. The relief coursed through the length of her body. He was all right. He was all right.

*   *   *

She lay back on the chesterfield, remembering she had promised to ring Emanuel Cellini. 'I'll do that in a moment,' she told herself. In a moment. When I've recovered. I will phone. Instead, she fell asleep as if drugged for more than an hour, to wake with a jolt to the sound of an Italian voice.

*   *   *

'There is a man downstairs asking for you,' said one of the servants.

'Send him up,' she said drowsily.

She was expecting Joshua, but the timid knock on the door was far from his style. She was utterly amazed, opening the living-room door, to see Emanuel Cellini, looking pale and dishevelled with stubble on his chin.

*   *   *

'I gave you my mother's notebooks,' he began without preliminary.

'Of course. They are quite safe,' she said defensively. 'I'm sorry I didn't call you back. I've had a bit of a shock.'

He shook his head impatiently.

'I *meant* to get back to you,' she said, taking in his complete lack of curiosity about her own troubles.

'The hotel said you were only booked in till this morning. I was afraid you might have left

256

with them.'

'You thought I'd *steal* them?'

She was appalled at this image of herself.

'Not exactly,' he said, hanging his head a little.

'You mean carelessly? As if they had no value?'

He shook his head.

'Of course not. But you *are* a journalist. I know that.'

'I see what you mean,' she said ruefully. 'Journalists do seem to be an unloved group of people, one way or another. However, the diaries are perfectly safe. I gave them to my friend for safekeeping.'

He stood where he was, looking at her as if still distrustful, as if he needed something else.

'You can check if you like,' she said impatiently.

'I am sure everything is there. But what did you think of them?'

*   *   *

She remembered the pain in them and tried to find something adequate to say.

'Extraordinary,' she said at last.

'You have understood, haven't you? That novel I put out as mine was a theft. From her.'

*   *   *

257

No wonder she had sensed the same hand behind journal and novel. It had been the same hand. She would have known about Beatrice as Giorgio's mistress. Yes. Correctly guessed she would dwindle as a wife. And the rest? Something between fantasy and fear.

'It was her *vision*,' she said slowly. *'Her* reading of Phaedra.'

'Yes.'

'Put her name on the next edition. You will have done her a service.'

'Ingrid Donkins wrote to my publisher, by the way. Ages ago. She said she used to be your father's agent. Do you trust her?'

'How do you mean?'

'To decide what should be done with them.'

'As to that,' said Rachel, 'she'll probably want to *sell* them. Is that what *you* want?'

'I don't know,' he said helplessly. 'I hoped you could tell me. My father used to say people would laugh at her writing. In a way, I've proved that isn't true. By what I did. But that was wrong, I know it was, and I'm trying to put it right. So you see . . .'

*   *   *

His voice trailed off, awkwardly. She looked at him, so crestfallen and frightened, taking this huge risk of coming to an almost unknown woman in a stranger's house; a boy frightened of intimacy to the point of sickness, turning to

258

her as to a mother.

'They won't laugh,' she said. 'You know that, don't you? But you might not want to expose them. Or her.'

He gave her a dark, grateful look.

'I haven't decided. I was hoping you could help me to guess how my mother would feel. I think she wanted me to do what I did. But this . . . this seems different.'

'Is there much more?'

'Oh yes. Trunkloads.'

'Then you can't let it moulder away to dust.'

*   *   *

Rachel remembered her own role with some embarrassment.

'Do you want me to write about all this?'

'My father—'

'Forget him.'

'*Yes*, then,' he said.

He seemed curious about her dismissal of Cellini.

'Did he hurt you?' he asked her.

'Nothing serious,' she said.

And she realised that was true.

'I'm *never* going to do that.'

'What?'

'Fall in love. It does such terrible things to people.'

'Yes, you will,' she said, without confidence.

'People are so damaged by it. If you can

manage *without*, why do it?'

'There's a story by Henry James,' she said, after a pause. 'Do you know it? "The Beast in the Jungle", I think it is. I haven't read it since I was at Cambridge.'

He shook his head.

'I haven't read any Henry James.'

'Well, I'm not sure I'm remembering it very exactly. There was a man who was afraid some terrible thing was going to happen to him. So he lived very carefully. All his life long. And nothing did. But then, right at the end of his life, he understood. That *was* the terrible thing.'

'I don't understand.'

'That *nothing* had happened,' she said. That was the terrible thing. That he'd felt nothing.'

'Do you think that is the worst thing? Not to feel?'

'Yes,' she said. 'The very worst. If you don't feel, you might as well be dead.'

*   *   *

He shook his head as if he were learning a difficult lesson.

'Do you care for someone?'

'Oh yes,' she said, remembering Tom and then thinking of Joshua, wondering why he hadn't rung back as he promised.

'And if I *don't*? If I *can't*?'

Suddenly she was frightened that she might

be telling him his life amounted to nothing, that he would throw it away if he believed her.

'I don't know. I'm not a therapist,' she said helplessly. 'You have to open yourself up to people.'

A long time seemed to pass as he thought about what she was saying.

'I think I'm too sick,' he said.

'Listen,' she said. 'You *aren't* sick. Your mother wasn't sick either. Just unhappy.'

'I don't know,' he said.

'Trust me,' she said. There *will* be people to love you.'

'I don't need to be loved,' he said. 'I just want to be liked.'

'Well, I like you,' she exclaimed.

'Do you?'

'Yes,' she said.

'I heard about your son. You must be very frightened for him.'

'Yes. I was but he's alright now.'

'So you must love him.'

'Very much.'

*   *   *

When Emanuel had gone, she looked at the silent telephone and puzzled about Joshua's silence. She rang down to ask the Embassy servants. There had been no calls. No messages.

*   *   *

Peter phoned from the civic reception on a mobile phone.

'It's quite amazing. Tom is free. I just heard. I'm afraid I don't have any details but it's all over.'

'Even better, I've spoken to him,' she said. 'He didn't say how it was managed, but he's flying home.'

'All the information I *had* suggested it was going to be a long haul, and I was preparing to say as much to you when I thought you could bear it. These things have been known to drag on for months. Even years. What will you do now?'

'Go back to the hotel and pack. Then fly to London.'

'Yes. Well, good luck. One of the drivers will take you, and I'll make sure your calls are transferred as soon as you leave.'

Thanks,' she said.

There was a pause.

'I don't know how the deal was cut,' said Peter. 'When you find out, would you let me know?'

She was puzzled herself, but not in any important part of her. Most of her attention was focused on getting back to London. Another part was speculating on what had happened to Joshua. And Emanuel's papers.

*   *   *

Back at her hotel, Rachel paid the bill by American Express. Then she arranged an early flight in the morning. When she'd packed her few clothes, she sat on the edge of the bed. She was tired, and had an ungrateful sense of flatness. After a few moment's hesitation, she picked up the telephone.

*   *   *

Joshua answered from his room at the third ring. He didn't sound surprised to hear her voice.

'You didn't phone,' she said, rather like a spoilt child.

'No.'

'I thought you were coming round?'

Tom's on his way back to England,' he said. 'As a matter of fact, I thought you'd be on a plane yourself by now.'

'Tom can't possibly get back to London until tomorrow afternoon,' she said. 'I asked the airport. It's a very long haul, plus he has to change at Singapore. So I shall still be at Heathrow before him, even if I catch the nine-thirty flight tomorrow morning.'

There was a pause.

'Listen,' she said. 'I've been wondering. If all the journalists had been pulled out of Padang, and the Foreign Office were digging

263

in, and nobody could get the local police to bother . . .'

'I got through on email,' he said.

'But who did you get through *to*?'

'An old student of Eng. Lit.,' said Joshua. 'Ten years ago he was in London writing a dissertation for Padang University on Somerset Maugham. Turns out Maugham is what people study as Modern British Literature. You may not remember this, but I once wrote a play about the fellow's last days.'

'I do remember. I saw it. Very funny,' she said impatiently.

'Well, so did he. Unusually smart fellow. He wanted to quote a bit. I think while he was in London he discovered a few things had happened over here since the thirties. At any rate, when he became head of a department in the University of Padang, he stayed in touch. When they went on to email, he gave me their address. I can't say I'd thought of using it before.'

'Email,' she repeated, still bewildered.

'Yes. I'm not sure the kind of freedom it permits will be allowed indefinitely. Authoritarian regimes won't be keen on the world wide web, and it's easy enough to police service providers.'

'But how did he help? This PhD student?'

'Professor, now,' he corrected her. 'And it was his brother-in-law who helped.'

There was something else she wanted to know but she had no words for it.

'It was very good of you to go to so much trouble,' she said.

He gave a bark of laughter.

'Be *sensible*, Rachel O'Malley.'

*   *   *

She could hear in his voice all the affectionate warmth of that evening on the Campo de'Fiori, but he had turned away from her then and put her in a taxi. She had no wish to invite another snub. She hesitated. Then she heard an exhalation of breath, something like a sigh.

'So I blew it,' he said. 'A moonlit walk, a Boy Scout confession . . .'

She could hear no irony in his voice.

'Out of character. Of course, you didn't understand a *word* I was saying.'

'Well . . .' she said.

'Now *did* you?'

'I thought I had.'

'Does inviting a girl to dinner sound like piss-off? Not really, wouldn't you say, if you'd done any thinking at all?'

'I'd like to see you,' she admitted.

'I'll be over in about ten minutes,' he said.

265

EPILOGUE

Joshua woke at seven and said into Rachel's ear, 'Don't sleep too long. It's about half an hour to the airport.'

His chin, black with stubble, scratched her shoulder.

'Those papers,' she said sleepily. 'The Cellini papers. I think they could be dynamite.'

'I *know* they are,' said Joshua smugly.

'You mean you've *read* them?'

'Yes. Neither of us are very moral, are we? I mean, you didn't keep your word, for instance.'

Rachel sat up at once. She had more or less decided neither to apologise nor explain.

'*How* did you know?'

'Well, I sat in my car outside your hotel most of the night and when you didn't come back, I guessed. All right, it was tricky of me not to admit I was guessing. I'm sorry.'

'I behaved with amazing stupidity,' said Rachel. 'Just tell me what you found.'

'Well, the poetry looked rather good, but it's the rest that will put paid to any chance of a Cabinet post for Cellini. I took copies—I hope you don't mind. One's in my bank vault; one I gave to MI5.'

'What kind of information could possibly interest MI5?'

'Links.'

'Twenty-year-old links?'

'She kept notes, you see. On the people who came to the house. Names. Physical descriptions. Dates. Cellini seems to have had a finger in every arms-dealing racket there's been a question mark over since the end of World War II. Plenty of the people are still around. Take it from me, Europol will be very interested.'

'But if Cellini guessed that, why . . .' she began.

'Of course he didn't guess that, or he would never have handed the papers over to Emanuel so meekly in the first place. He only felt endangered after the novel came out. He knew no one could legitimately refuse him political office on the strength of a novel but he had a kind of instinct there might be something else that would tie him to the story if the press got their hands on his wife's notebooks. Something that his political enemies could use. That's why it was worth his while to lean on the singer a little. I say nothing of any other pursuit, by the way.'

'Good,' she said. 'Let's not.'

*   *   *

Rachel smiled at the man in reception, and handed him the card for her room.

'Is there a taxi for me?' she asked. 'I

ordered it last night.'

'Right outside,' he said. 'And this came for you.'

Rachel stared at the A4 envelope, puzzled. She didn't recognise the handwriting and could think of no one from whom she expected to hear. With a quick glance at the clock, she tore it open. Inside were a few typed pages, whose style she could see at once resembled that of Emanuel's novel. There was no other clue, no note that she could see. I'll read it on the plane, she told herself.

*　　　*　　　*

On the plane, she read the English paper and thought of Joshua. It came to her that she had fallen in love with a man she actually *liked*. It was decidedly a new development. Maybe we'll be happy for a bit, she thought to herself. She thought of happiness almost as a childhood garden with high pear trees and raspberry bushes and sunshine on the grass. Something across a wall, through a door to which she didn't have the key, that she had learnt to live sturdily without needing. Most people she knew lived outside. It was tempting to imagine it possible to go in.

*　　　*　　　*

Her thoughts wandered to her mother,

somewhere bravely making her way about the world essentially alone. She felt a pang of sadness for her, untinged with usual self-pity and resentment. How much of the chilliness between them had been of her own making? She was uncertain. She had failed to reach her with the news of Tom's release, and delegated the task to Anna. That seemed inadequate now to the love and fear she had heard in her mother's voice. She hoped Christopher had heard the conclusion of the Sumatra incident and decided he must have; he would otherwise have been still frantic. When she arrived home, she must telephone to reassure him. Somehow, he no longer seemed to threaten an emotional quagmire.

*   *   *

And underneath all that network of thoughts and half-thoughts pattering about her brain was the single, solid knowledge of Tom travelling at that very moment towards London and safety. Rachel was so centrally aware of this miracle that some superstitious part of her refused to let herself imagine his quick grin and unsentimental kiss. Instead, she wondered what Tom would make of Joshua when he came on a visit, and concluded they might get on. Tom might even be glad to see another man in the house. She was sitting in a window seat. It was a very blue day; clear except for a few wisps of white cloud far on the western horizon; she could see the coastline of northern Italy, and a line of mountains rising into whiteness. Over the loudspeaker came the captain's voice: the flight should be smooth and comfortable but he was sorry to say the weather was reported to be cold and windy in London.

*   *   *

'Did you have a good trip?'

Looking up, startled, Rachel recognised the black athlete she had met on the way out.

'Great,' she said, smiling. 'And you?'

'Fine,' he said. 'That's really a cool city.'

'Did you win?' she asked.

'Yes, I did,' he responded, with a huge smile. 'Things going okay for you?'

She nodded, and they parted with the cheery bonhomie of those who at least for a moment number themselves among the fortunate of this earth.

*   *   *

The half-remembered words of Marcus Aurelius, whose horse she had spent so long examining in the Capitoline museum a few days ago, came back to her: 'It makes no difference whether you live thirty thousand years, or thirty, all you have to lose is the

271

present moment.'

*   *   *

So then I should *savour* this present moment, she thought: this unlooked for serenity; the coffee with its bitterness muted by cream; the chocolate with its mint centre making the sweetness palatable. She looked out at the gleam on the shoreline along the flat pond of the Mediterranean; relished the sensation of flying above so green and hospitable a planet. She was not in pain, not anxious, not unhappy. She had an article to write that had almost as many question marks in it as known facts: but she could do it, she thought, without fudging the uncertainties, without pretending to know more than she did. She travelled in this pleasant way for about half an hour before suddenly remembering the manilla envelope in her white bag. She retrieved the bag from the locker above her head, then impatiently drew out the typed pages and settled down to read.

My dearest Emanuel
These are my dreams. I give them to you. Do what you like with them. Add your own truth. Put them out in the world, if you like. For me, but not under my name. Already I know you will do whatever you think is right. That you love me.

Giorgio will marry again. Why should he not? I

am no longer jealous of that, though once the thought tormented more than any other. It is only of you, my son, that I feel possessive. Don't misunderstand me. When I think of you grown and happy, with a wife who will look after you, I am not jealous of her love in the least. It is only when I think of another woman pretending to be your mother, taking away from me the child I know now with your fair hair and your thoughtful grey eyes like my own. Then I confess I am unhappy.

You will not read this until you are grown up and it cannot damage you. Or perhaps all the damage will have already been done to you and not by me.

If you knew what I wished for you, my darling. But I shall not be there to see what becomes of you. If there is any protection a soul can offer from beyond the grave, you shall have mine. Who knows whether there is not some truth in the tales we scoff at? Human beings all over the world have comforted themselves with similar nonsense. I am not a natural believer. If I try to imagine myself living behind your curtains, an invisible intelligence, watching over you helplessly, fuming over the waste of your beauty and your spirit, it doesn't seem likely. Yet I swear, if dry bones can, I shall raise myself out of the soil to damage anyone who raises a hand against you.

Rachel put the pages away, and began to cry silently. Her eyes were still wet when the plane took its place in the queue of planes waiting to land at Heathrow.

We hope you have enjoyed this Large Print book. Other Chivers Press or Thorndike Press Large Print books are available at your library or directly from the publishers.

For more information about current and forthcoming titles, please call or write, without obligation, to:

Chivers Press Limited
Windsor Bridge Road
Bath BA2 3AX
England
Tel. (01225) 335336

OR

Thorndike Press
295 Kennedy Memorial Drive
Waterville
Maine 04901
USA

All our Large Print titles are designed for easy reading, and all our books are made to last.

scuttled